Have fun,
watch for
Sandy Compton

Archer MacClehan

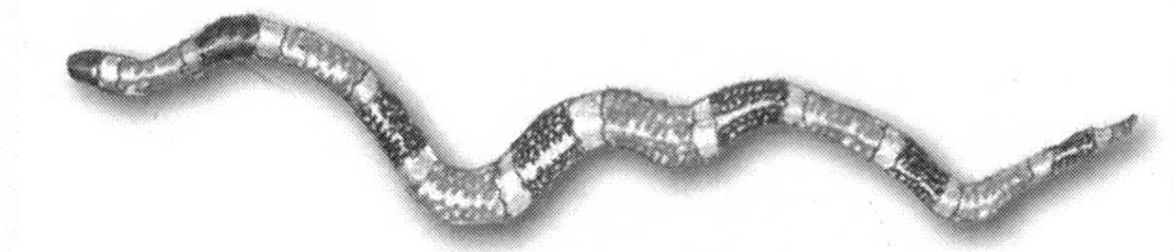

and The Girl Who Wouldn't Stop Running

by

SANDY COMPTON

Manufactured in the United States of America

ISBN 978-1-886591-16-5

Library of Congress Control Number: 2014933192

$15.00 — Copies of this book may be purchased at your local bookstore, online at www.bluecreekpress.com, at amazon.com or from Blue Creek Press by writing to books@bluecreekpress.com

Heartfelt thanks to my friends Gary Payton and Bob Lange for their kind remarks and essential criticisms.

Archer MacClehan & The Girl Who Wouldn't Stop Running
is a **Blue Mobius Book** from

Blue Creek Press
Box 110 • Heron, Montana • 59844
www.bluecreekpress.com
books@bluecreekpress.com

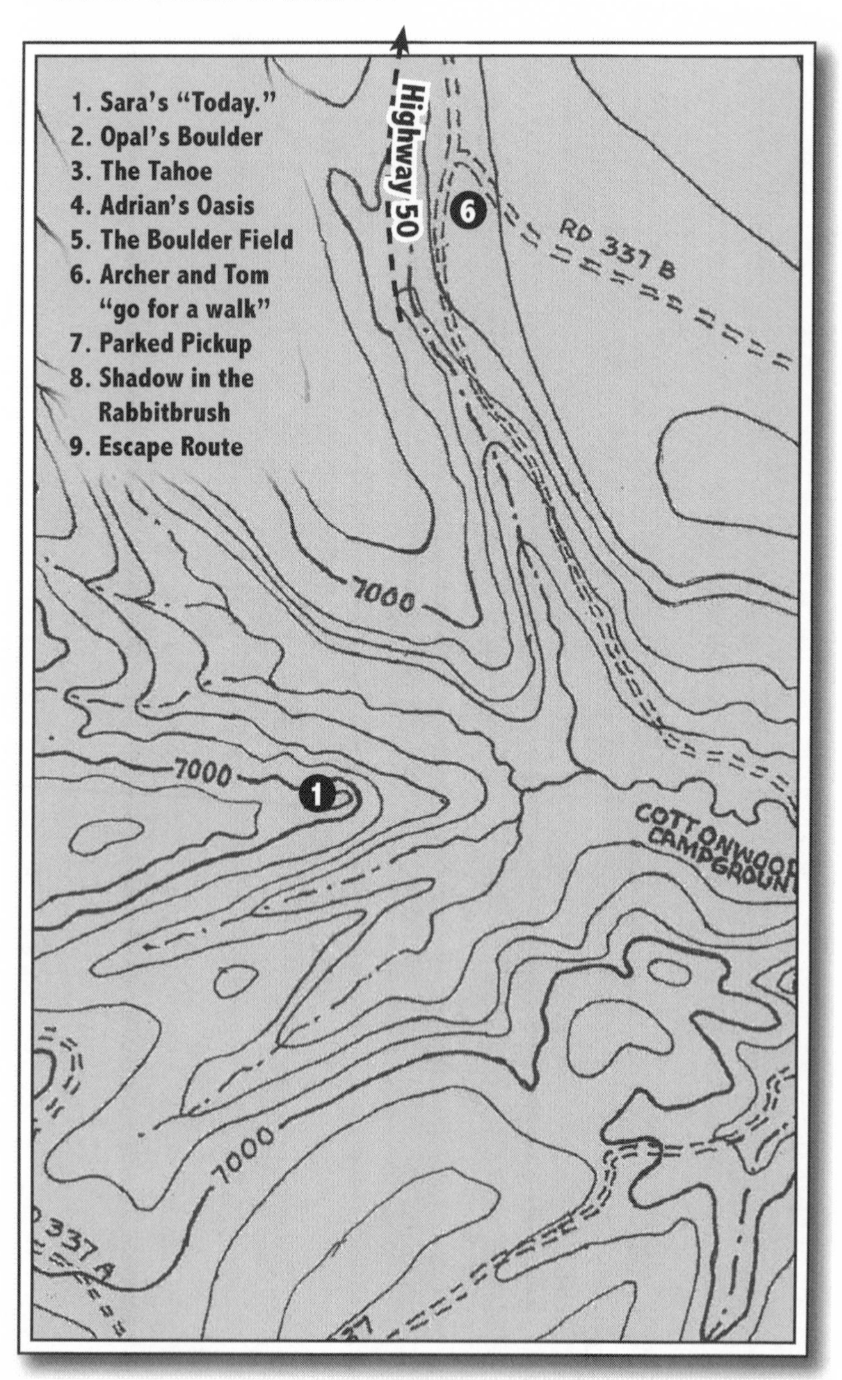
1. Sara's "Today."
2. Opal's Boulder
3. The Tahoe
4. Adrian's Oasis
5. The Boulder Field
6. Archer and Tom "go for a walk"
7. Parked Pickup
8. Shadow in the Rabbitbrush
9. Escape Route
Highway 50
RD 337 B
7000
7000
7000
COTTONWOOD CAMPGROUND
337A

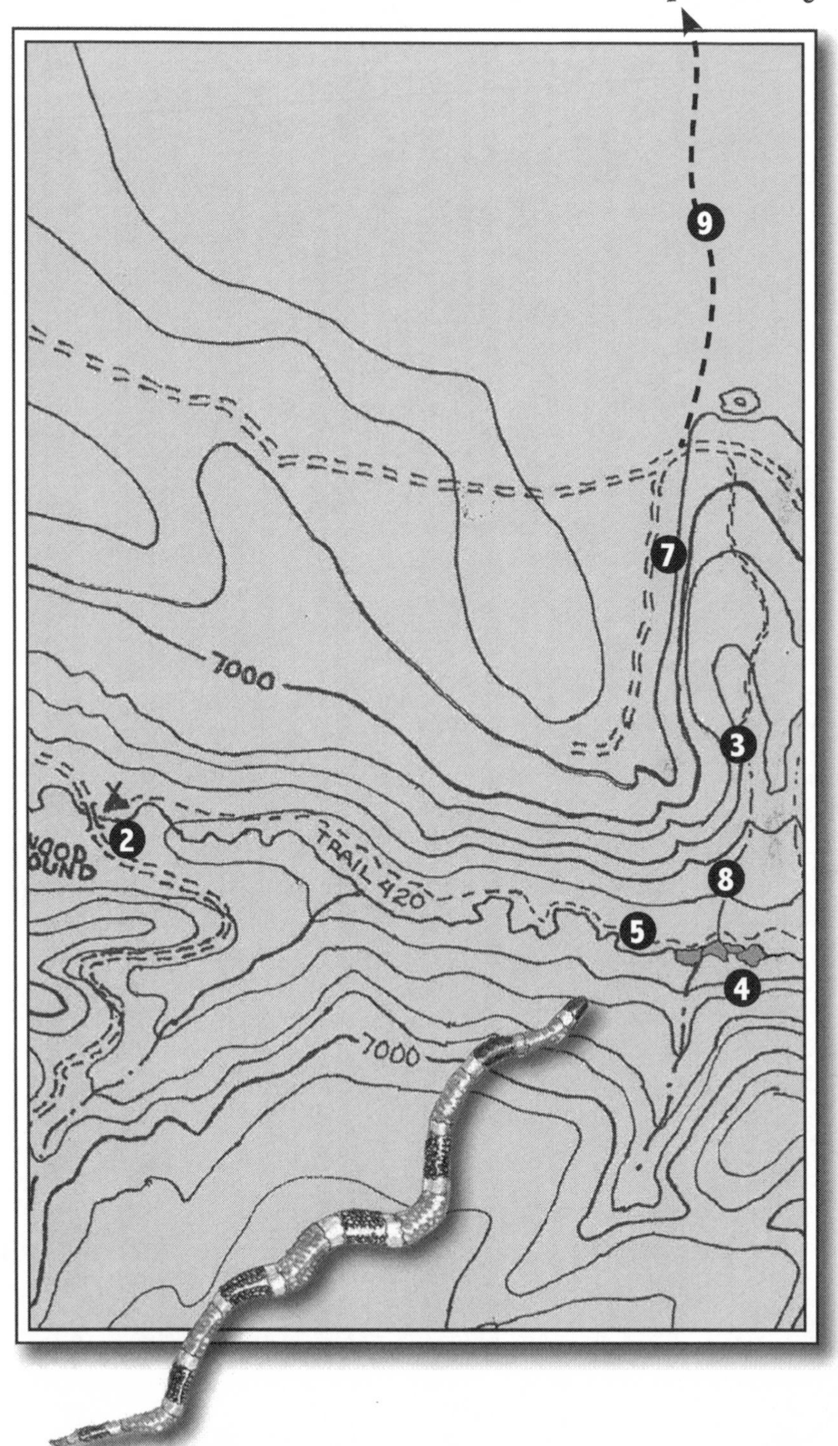
9
7
7000
3
2
TRAIL 420
8
5
4
7000

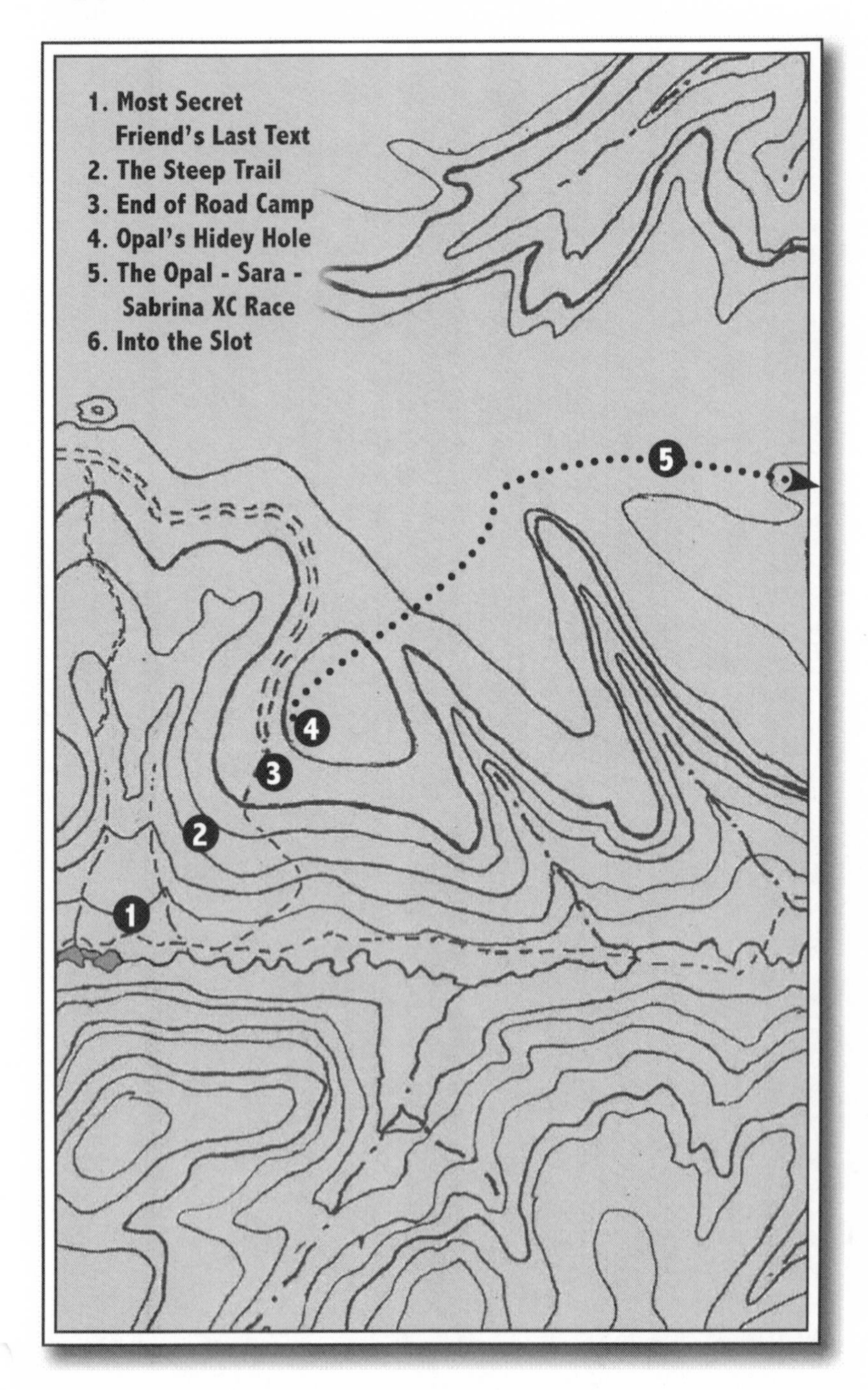
1. Most Secret Friend's Last Text
2. The Steep Trail
3. End of Road Camp
4. Opal's Hidey Hole
5. The Opal - Sara - Sabrina XC Race
6. Into the Slot
5
4
3
2
1

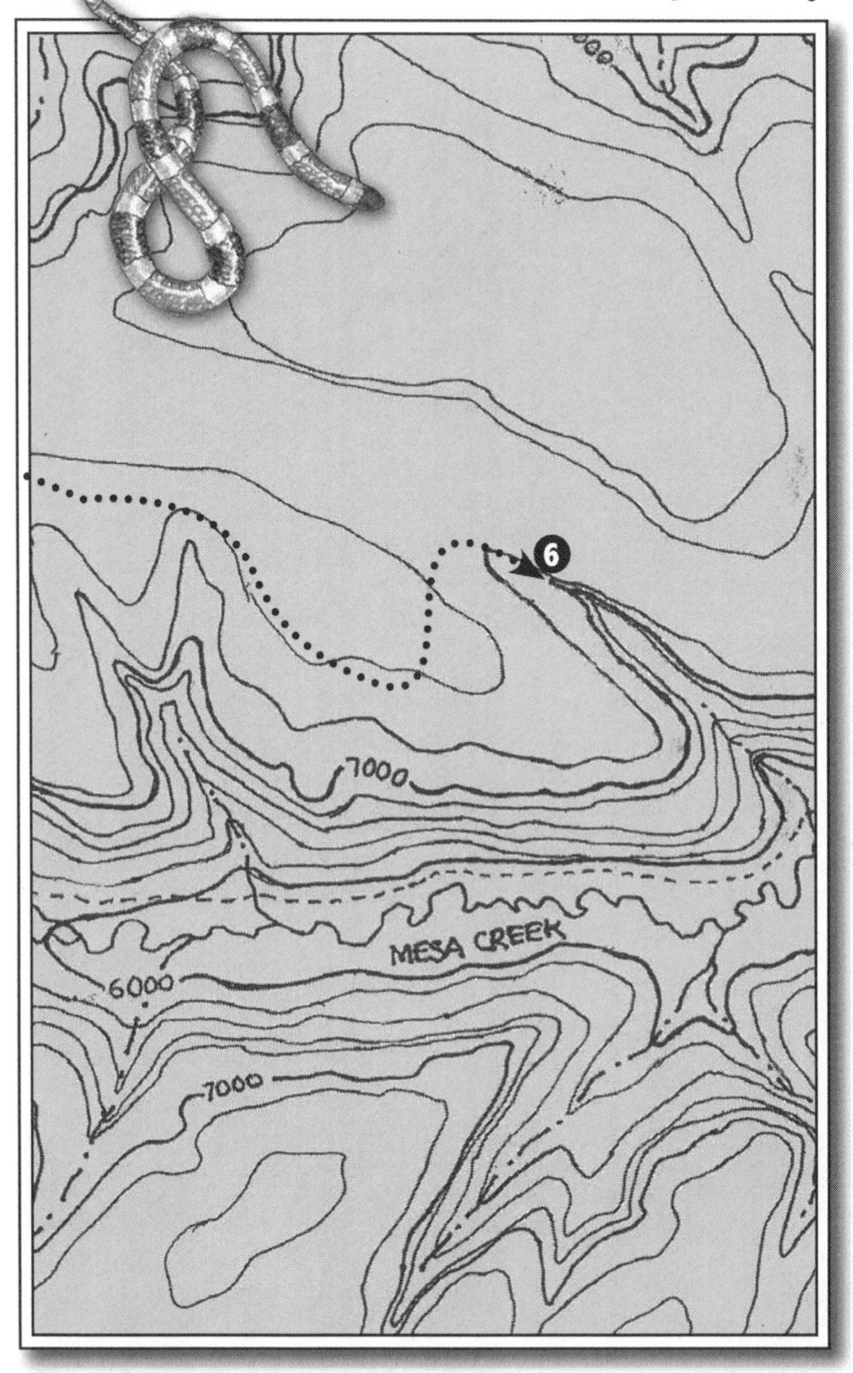
6
7000
MESA CREEK
6000
7000

For that girl who ain't a girl, whoever she might be.

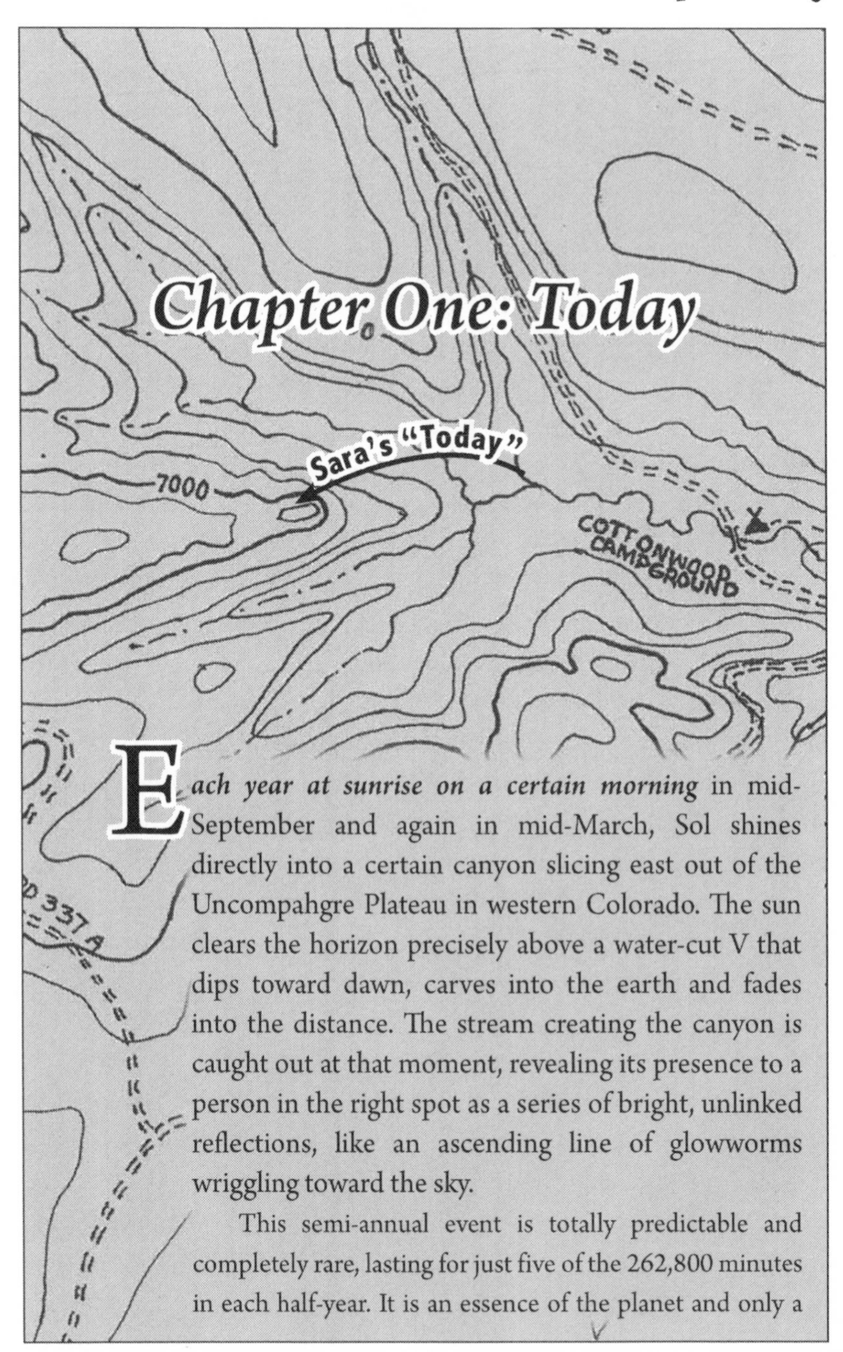

Chapter One: Today

Each year at sunrise on a certain morning in mid-September and again in mid-March, Sol shines directly into a certain canyon slicing east out of the Uncompahgre Plateau in western Colorado. The sun clears the horizon precisely above a water-cut V that dips toward dawn, carves into the earth and fades into the distance. The stream creating the canyon is caught out at that moment, revealing its presence to a person in the right spot as a series of bright, unlinked reflections, like an ascending line of glowworms wriggling toward the sky.

This semi-annual event is totally predictable and completely rare, lasting for just five of the 262,800 minutes in each half-year. It is an essence of the planet and only a lucky few witness it. Of those, even fewer perceive the gift they receive. Sara Cafferty, who was in that certain spot on that certain morning, took note of it and knew it for what it was.

When the moment came, she was tapping away with her favorite Estwing rock hammer at a chunk of aggregate broken from a tower of the stuff lying fallen, shattered and scattered across a yellowish sandstone bench that rolled out to an edge 25 yards away and disappeared. She was trying to decipher the contents of the aggregate and thereby get a look into the past.

Sara's morning was that one leaning toward the Autumnal equinox. She was there early because on some days — even in mid September —it is egg-frying hot on that bench by 11 o'clock, and she wished to be somewhere less exposed by that time. Sara, who is slender and freckled and redheaded and not tall and tougher than the casual observer might suspect in a variety of ways physical and otherwise, had been watching the sun clear the horizon from close to that certain spot for over a week. She had noted its progress as it worked its way daily further south along the jagged line that is the eastern edge of this world; a long way off, indeed.

Even though the gift was absolutely unexpected, it was completely appreciated, for Sara knew by the laws of planetary movement that the sight she was seeing would not recur the next day. She took several pictures, and knew they would not do justice even as she pushed the button.

These are some of the things that Sara Cafferty — recovering adult child of privilege, seeker, geology student and expat from big business — knew on that convergent day in September. What she didn't know as she tried to discern the distant past by reading rocks was her immediate future, which was a good thing. Brave as she was, she might have run completely away.

Instead, she stood watch until the moment was over, sketching shadows in her notebook as fast as she could She knew she couldn't capture the light, but only leave it to fall where it would on her paper and on the rest of the world. Her only chance was to ignore it and let it settle to earth of its own volition, and this made her think of Archer MacClehan.

Go away, thought, she thought

A related thought sprang forth uninvited. Among the bits of wisdom the study of geology had imprinted upon Sara was the ephemerality of all things. "Nothing is forever," Dr. Albertson had said perhaps a million million times—a terabyte of nothing-is-forever's.

This was, in Sara's quick and quirky mind, Albertson's Second Postulate. Albertson's First Postulate, which was her favorite Albertsonian theory, was the Stardust Postulate. This was the possibility that the preponderance of Precambrian rock could, just as easily as not, be an accretion of stardust; that the formative planet might have flown for a million centuries through the detritus of an exploded star, some of which came aboard and sank into the primordial seas. This would be, when proved, the Albertsonian Period of the Precambrian Eon.

Dr. Albertson was one of the most creative thinkers Sara Cafferty knew, quite unlike some of his more fact-bound colleagues. Part of his secret was an ability to see incredible distances into the past and future and then compress time into unforgettable visual modern analogies.

"The planet," he asserted, "is a crumpled-up ball of temporary seas and wayward continents, a spinning, formative changeup slow curve flung by Something-Or-Other on an oval trajectory around another crumpled-up ball that happens to be on fire and moving in its own oval trajectory around, perhaps, that same Who-Knows-What."

Sara always saw "Something-Or-Other" and "Who-Knows-What" as capitalized. After taking a number of classes from Dr. Albertson and having him as her current thesis advisor, she understood that was how he referenced God.

Sara loved Dr. Albertson for his hyperbole, among other things. Some tiny part of her wished that she had met him before there was a Mrs. Albertson, but that would have been when she was 12 years old and still climbing Vulture Peak on a regular basis. That was bMBA (before her Masters in Business Administration), and bRT (before Rob Thorsen, former fiancé), and definitely bAMC (before Archer MacClehan). And, ouch, that hurt, thinking of Mr. MacClehan twice in the same morning — dang his lovely, scarred-up hide. She looked north and caught herself at it. She wished to share this treasured five minutes with the person she privately called the lead dog, for she had a good idea that he would recognize the gift also. In fact, she longed . . .

No longing! she emphatically told herself. *It's been too long to long.*

How long had it been? *Too blinkin' long,* she thought.

"Well, what are you waiting for?" she asked herself out loud. She often asked this.

Something she knew not what. Only that Something-Or-Other had been saying, "Not yet."

She turned the Estwing over and drove the point into the aggregate, cleaving off a chunk as big as her head, which she admonished to just be quiet and let her think about rock. She flipped the tool back to the hammer side and began to bang away at the concretion, reducing it to hunks of somewhat unrelated stone. Most of it was rounded by stream wear, some was igneous, some was sedimentary. A very little of it was metamorphic.

"Where, oh, where did you all come from?" she sang to the pebbles and cobbles and sand she quarried from the aggregate. She brought out a notebook and began to catalog the rubble. Quartzite. Granite. Mudstone. Siltstone. She frowned. No sandstone.

"Hmmm." It got very quiet. The sun climbed into the sky. Sara moved deeper into the rock, intent on trying to see where this stuff had grown and how it had gotten to where it was now.

Once, she thought she heard a shout from far away. She frowned and looked at her watch and cocked her head to listen, but it was as if it had come from another universe. It did not recur. The puzzle reabsorbed her, brought her to center in a place she loved to be — within the Great Mystery, as she called it — leaching small clues out of the planet to be filed next to other clues she had already gathered, all having to do with "where did this thing come from and how did it get *here*?"

The sun was warm on her back. The hiss and burble of the creek running over stone 120 feet beneath the edge of the bench rose to her. A breeze rustled a stand of aspen in a side canyon. The first cicada of the day began to sing. Then — so clearly that it startled her; nearly scared her — she heard Something-Or-Other say, "Today."

"Excuse me?"

"Today."

Today, she thought. *Just like that. OK. Fine.*

A big butterfly settled behind her solar plexus, a huge yellow and black monarch moving its wings in time to her heart. She focused on not letting it move its wings too fast. She made herself finish cataloging the aggregate and put her tools and notebook and sketchbook away in her pack. She took a big drink of water. She ate some trail mix. She checked on the butterfly. Still there.

She looked at her watch again. To her surprise, it was already 9 o'clock. *Mountain Time,* she thought. And it was definitely time to go make that call. Not only today, but now.

Deliberately, she began back toward the pickup, an hour's hike up the canyon.

"I will not run," she said. "It will be too hot to run," she told herself. But, she wanted to run.

When she got to the truck, it would be at least another 45 minutes to a place where her cell phone worked with any reliability. There was an urge to hurry, but there was no hurrying up this trail, just as there would be no hurrying along the two-lane track that passed for a road.

Today, she thought, and took another step up the trail.

Chapter Two: Grandpa Joe

T*hree days before Sara's "Today"* and far north of the dancing glowworms, a big, high wing, single-engine Kodiak with six souls aboard flew a line toward a single, sinistral needle of smoke stuck into the dome of an ultramarine sky. The world a thousand feet below the plane was emerald, kelly, vert, moss and celadon — every manner of green — clinging in a never-ending variety of conic forms to contorted, mounded, eroded and ice-chiseled stone.

In the left front seat of the Kodiak was the man Sara Cafferty thought of as the lead dog. He scanned the western edge of the world. Seven miles away, a little wind leaned the needle north, and the lead dog was glad it was little. Archer MacClehan didn't like people launching themselves out of his airplane when the wind was being unruly.

Flying with the back door off made light conversation impossible, so the passengers said nothing they didn't mean. As the sky blew by the big opening on the starboard side, they busied themselves checking straps, maps, packs and equipment bags.

Archer spoke into his mouthpiece, and the man in the jump seat beside the missing door heard, "Three minutes to the zone."

Joe Skladany nodded. In best jumpmaster fashion he yelled at the four passengers, "THREE MINUTES." One responded with a thumb's up, and the four of them pulled chest straps tighter nearly as a unit.

"Holey samoley!" crackled in the jumpmaster's ears. "Cover that mike before you yell, Joe, or I'll dump *you* out the door, too."

"Jeez. Sorry, AJ."

"It's not as if you've never done this before, Joe."

" 'K. You're right. Sorry."

Joe Skladany felt foolish. It was a greenhorn's trick to yell into the headset mic, and he was no greenhorn, though he felt as antsy as one today. This was probably the last jump of the fire season for all of them, and possibly the last he would ever participate in. He wasn't quite sure yet how he felt about that.

"It's a piece of cake, Joe," advised his headphones. "Piece of cake."

Joe pulled himself into his center and felt a familiar calm settle inside. MacClehan was in the left seat, and these kids — a reference to that approaching retirement — knew the drill. No newbees. Turnbull and Smith out on the first pass, Sevlakovs and Slater on the second. Toss the tools and food out on the third. Two of the four wearing parachutes moved gingerly from their seats to near Joe and assumed a sprinter's "ready" stance, on one knee with one foot under them.

He pointed at the jumpers, motioned them closer to the open door, made sure they hooked to the static line.

"Ninety seconds," said his headset.

He unstrapped and stood to put his hand on the first jumper's shoulder and pulled him around into the door, then knelt with his hand on the jumper's right calf. He pulled the mic under his chin. Beneath the plane, individual spruce and mountain hemlock raced at 140 miles per hour in the opposite direction, as if trying to escape the fire Archer was homing on.

The ridge-top clearing they had chosen for the jump zone was coming up fast — one, and, two, and — "GO!" he yelled, and pushed the smokejumper out the door.

The next jumper stepped into the door. Joe slapped her calf — "GO!" She screamed as if she was about to die, as she always did when she went out, and, as always, it made Joe laugh.

Jesse Turnbull was a funny gal, in a number of ways. She characterized herself as tall for her age, which was "somewhere north of 30," she admitted. She had surprising gray eyes and short-cropped dark hair shot through with red and silver highlights. Her lanky frame, angular build, high cheekbones and wide mouth might have qualified her as a model had she wanted to be one, but she would much rather jump out of airplanes, fight fires and do other "boy stuff" than strut down a runway.

Joe pulled the mic up and got back into the jump seat beside the door. "Two gone."

"Hang on, then," his headset advised him, and he got his belt on before the Kodiak hauled hard to port and began around for another pass.

As the plane heeled over, a small and anomalous vibration on the starboard side worked its way into the struts and then into the aluminum skin of the wing. From there, it jumped into an aileron and then ran down the cable that attached it to the controls of the pilot. So slight, it was as if one voice in the Mormon Tabernacle Choir was singing off key. It was not so much felt as sensed by the man in the left seat.

He frowned at the feeling and pulled his headset off. The wind blowing through the plane made it hard to hear, but he listened as best as he could. There was no telltale flutter in the sound of the passage of the plane through the air. As he leveled the plane out, the feeling went away.

He made for the back turn so they could get the rest of the firefighters on the ground.

Tom Sevlakovs and Joe Skladany both saw Archer pull his headset off. They exchanged a glance, each wearing a similar small frown of concern.

Archer MacClehan didn't take his headset off in mid-flight for no particular reason, particularly a flight where people were jumping out of his airplane.

Tom opened his hands and raised his eyebrows, a silent question. Joe answered with the same gesture. Archer put his headset back on.

"What's up, AJ?" Joe asked his mic.

"Nothing serious, Joe. I think we have something a little loose in the right wing, 'sall. We'll get home after we deliver the rest of our load."

If it had been any other pilot Joe Skladany flew with as jumpmaster, he would have been worried, but he knew the affinity Archer MacClehan had with any airplane he piloted. It was almost as if he put them on — no, he implanted himself into the airplane, became somehow part of it. He could sense things in a plane no other pilot Joe had ever ridden with could. And, if Archer said they would get home, Joe had no doubt that they would. He gave Tom a thumbs-up and Tom grinned and rolled his eyes in mock panic.

The Kodiak made the two additional passes necessary to drop the smokejumpers and their equipment and then flew across them again to make sure they were good to go. From the ground, Tom Sevlakovs waved them on and Archer hauled the plane to port and set course for base.

Joe plunked himself into the right seat, and settled in to enjoy the half-hour ride home.

"How's Opal doin,' Joe," his headset asked him.

Joe grinned.

"Drivin' her momma crazy, I think."

"How so?"

"Helen's got a guy she's sweet on, and Opal's doin' everything she can to keep them from — well, she's doin' her best to be protectin' her dad's interest."

"That must be hard."

"It's downright amusing!" Joe laughed.

Archer didn't answer. He knew Kelly and Helen Skladany had been through a nasty divorce and Joe was not good at staying neutral. He was a fiercely loyal father. If he believed his former daughter-in-law had any good reason to divorce his son, he was not admitting it.

Archer had an opinion, but he knew it was none of his business, so he kept it to himself.

Joe heard the silence, though, and looked at his friend. Straight, black hair cut short, eyes the same color as the sky, skin a shade darker than his eyes seemed to indicate, and a finely cast nose that left his brow and traveled in a slight downward arc to its pointed tip. A mouth that was wide, with full lips over a mouthful of good, white teeth — not perfect, but not too much worse for a high school and college football career. His chin seemed purely Scot ... or maybe Norwegian.

Though Archer's crooked grin was one of the most infectious Joe had ever seen, his mouth showed not a hint of it.

"Not funny?" Joe asked.

Archer didn't answer, but he gave his friend a wry little smile.

Joe Skladany looked out the starboard window, thinking of his beloved granddaughter Opal, and trying not to think about the divorce that had torn up her family and his. Helen, Opal and "the boyfriend" had just left for a Colorado vacation. He had hoped Opal would come stay with him — and knew that she wanted to — but Helen had insisted she go to Colorado with them. It was a mother's right, Joe conceded, but he still wished Opal had come to Montana.

Helen would soon feel the same way.

Chapter Three: Opal at Thirteen

On the evening before Sara's "Today," while she was off for a run in the cool of the evening, Ross Halliday sorted necessities into his pack — water bottles, trail mix, power bars, an apple, sunscreen, first aid kit, snakebite kit. His goal for the next day was to hike as far as he could before it got unbearably hot into the Colorado canyon where he was camped with Joe Skladany's ex-daughter-in-law Helen and granddaughter Opal. The camp in which he was sorting necessities was a cottonwood-studded oasis straddling the stream that would mutate into glowworms for Sara the next morning.

The odds against this coincidence are relatively high, but not as high as those of Sara being in the right place at the right time to observe the glowworms. Neither are they nearly as high as those against events that will unfold over the next few days in the lives of Sara, the folks in the camp ground, several occupants of Archer's airplane and a few players to be named later. But odds are sometimes to be beaten, as Opal would soon demonstrate to Ross.

Ross hoped Opal would hike with him, the odds of which he knew were incalculably low even as he asked her. As she often did, Opal demonstrated by a single look that Ross' presence on *her* planet was completely unacceptable, and she would be pleased when he finally fell off. This did not hurt his feelings as it once might have, but it did add to his pile of frustrations with the girl. He bit his tongue and made ready to go alone.

Helen knew that some activity like a long hike together was key to getting Ross and Opal on the right track — finally. She was also close to sick of both her daughter *and* her boyfriend on the tenth day of their vacation, and was not lying when she said, "Why don't you go with Ross on his hike, Opal? I need a little time alone."

Opal, on the other hand, *was* lying when she said, "'Cause I don't want to," She really *did* want to, but it involved a compromise she had promised herself — "cross my heart and hope to die" — she would never make.

"Opal. . . ." Helen's voice held the familiar edge of a threat. When she heard it in herself, she stopped and looked at her daughter. Opal was taller every day, it seemed, stretching herself right out of her baby fat. She braided her own hair now, an auburn plait pulled straight back from her wide, honest face and exposing protruding, round little ears set low on her head. Her eyes came from the Skladany side: hazel with flecks of green and almost too close together on opposite sides of an upturned nose with a herd of freckles crossing its divide. Braces were working on the Johnson-gene overbite, the one that had earned Helen orthodontic work as a girl, too.

Helen knew Opal was not going to be the most beautiful woman in the world, but boys were already lining up to talk to her, which concerned Helen a little but not a lot. She trusted her daughter even when she was being difficult — and she was being difficult. At thirteen years old, living in a split world where accountability was limited by her next move to the other parent's home, Opal was very good at being difficult.

"I really wish you'd go, Opal," Helen said. "I need a little space, and I don't need to be fighting with you about anything."

Opal, as much as she wanted to, just couldn't. Sometimes, and especially lately, she felt her loathing of Ross eroding, and this made it even more imperative to be difficult about Ross. Even though her mother liked Ross Halliday a lot, Opal's loyalty to her father dictated that she couldn't like Ross Halliday at all. It was her strategy to be uncooperative regarding Ross at all times in hopes that he would go away and leave them alone. It was something Helen hoped her daughter would eventually outgrow, but she had been hoping that for over a year, and it seemed farther from possibility with each passing month.

"Why can't you just accept him," Helen had asked Opal more than a few times, "and let us have some peace when the three of us are together?"

"Why can't you just not see him when I'm with you?" Opal nearly always answered.

The rest of the conversation was most often a variation of the following:

"I like to be with Ross," Helen would say. "He's my boyfriend. We enjoy each other's company. We like to do things together. We'd like to do things with you."

"I don't think so," Opal would retort. "Rot would rather not ever see me."

"That's not true, Ope." Helen had given up on insisting she not call him "Rot." "He loves you as much as he loves me."

"Don't make me gag. And my name is Opal."

"I know what your name is. I gave it to you." Helen's voice would drop and grow a hard edge. Through set teeth, she might say, "I won't have you treating me this way or insulting Ross. I've had it with your insolence. You can go to your room and stay there until you apologize."

Opal never argued and very seldom had to apologize. She wanted to sing out as she ran up the stairs, "Born and bred in the briar patch," as Br'er Rabbit did after Br'er Fox finally threw him there. Her room was sanctuary, where she spent much of her time when she was at her mother's house. There, she could read, text her friends and avoid dealing with the reality of Ross.

Opal had two rooms to which she could be sent, one at each parent's; and they were remarkably different. At her mother's house, her room overlooked a well-aged Seattle street with Norway maples reaching for each other from the parking strips. The room was painted pale blue, a color Helen's therapist counseled her to choose so that it might have a calming influence on her daughter. However, a red maple outside the window filtered all light that entered, casting a rosy hue into the room on sunny summer days, This worried Helen when she was initially being paranoid about Opal's post-divorce mental health, but Helen's own mental health was such that she knew she was just being paranoid. She did not have the tree cut down.

Opal's bed was adorned with a white and blue quilted coverlet. The dresser and floor were populated by a family of stuffed elephants of varied sizes, ranging from Pogo —who was purple and bigger than Opal — down to Alice — who was a faded violet and fit in Opal's coat pocket.

Alice was Opal's favorite and Alice traveled a lot. Alice was the only elephant that went to stay with the stuffed bears that lived in her other room at Kelly Skladany's house five hours and a ferry ride away on the Washington coast. That room, which she was seldom banished to, had walls of blonde wood and a ceiling with a galaxy painted on it in glow-in-the-dark paint. The windows were French doors opening onto Opal's own balcony, where she could hear and see the surging Pacific. The bed was covered with a faded Hudson's Bay blanket, teal and ochre and yellow and red. It had once belonged to Opal's grandpa Joe, until she had taken a liking to it on a visit to his house in Montana. The blanket was frayed at the edges from years of service, with a hole Grandpa Joe told her was made by sleeping too close to a campfire when he was a young Forest Service trail-maker and sometimes firefighter on that same Olympic Peninsula where her father's house now sat.

The bears in Opal's room at her dad's house were less whimsical than the elephants. There were no purple or violet bears, just brown and black. Bubba was bigger than Pogo. Li'l Smokey was about the same size as Alice, but didn't travel much. He had belonged to Grandpa Joe, too, and was old and fragile.

Opal was not an unhappy child. She knew she had a good life, because she saw how other girls sometimes live when she went with her mom to the homeless shelter in downtown Seattle. But she also knew she could not like Rot Hellishday, which was her most secret name for Ross — she only shared it with Most Secret Friend during text sessions late at night. She wanted her mom and dad to kiss and make up, and Rot was making that more impossible all the time. So she kept to her strategy, even though she knew it made her mom crazy.

In the meantime, her mom and Ross tolerated Opal's obstinacy as they could and enjoyed the days when she was with her father; two weeks out of four, Thanksgiving, Fourth of July and every other Christmas.

On the other hand, Opal was very tolerant of her father's girlfriend. Sabrina was funny and fun and won Opal over quite easily, particularly since Kelly and Sabrina planned the meeting as a "chance encounter" *after* it had become apparent Helen was dating Ross; and *after* Opal had complained to her father that her mother had a boyfriend. In fact, Opal had intimated, though rather obliquely, that if her mom was going to have a boyfriend, maybe her dad should get a girlfriend — just to get even, you know — and maybe that girlfriend should be Sabrina.

What Opal's mom wasn't telling her, even though it caused Helen to remain in the role of "bad guy," was that Sabrina Jacklin might be funny and fun but she also had questionable taste in men. What woman in her right mind would be interested in a man who'd left his wife for another woman — even if she *was* the woman he'd left his wife for. Helen never complained directly to Opal about her father's behavior and never, ever knowingly impugned Kelly's — or Sabrina's — reputation. She was smarter than that. Helen went out of her way to make sure she didn't get between Opal and her dad. She figured one broken heart per household was plenty. Opal's might be dented but it wasn't torn in half like hers.

W***hy Helen wasn't telling*** was multifold, including the shame of being cuckolded, truth be told, but the main reason was that she loved her daughter enough to not ruin her relationship with her father even at the expense of her own. She knew Opal would grow up someday. When that happened, Helen wanted to always be able to look Opal in the eye and know that she had done her best by her.

Chapter Four: Bad Buys

Four miles away — as the vulture flies — from Cottonwood Campground and a steep three-quarters of a mile from the stream of the ascending glowworms, a beat-up gray Chevy Tahoe sat deep in a tributary canyon accessed by a nearly impassable and unofficial road. It was as far down the canyon as the driver dared take it, which was a ways, for he was daring — and good — at driving off-road. When he could go no further, he tucked the Tahoe — pointed uphill — under an overhang against the west wall of the slot, taking advantage of the growing afternoon shade. It looked instantly like it had been rusting away there for a decade.

The Chevy was much more mechanically sound than it looked. A knowing assessment of its tires might cause the assessor to wonder why someone driving such a decrepit vehicle would buy such good tread. Though fully earned, the Tahoe's dents and scrapes and dowdy appearance were an intentional ruse, as were the Nevada plates and the camping and prospecting equipment piled neatly in the back. Under the dust, rust and damaged skin, the Tahoe was, as the driver asserted, "a brute."

The driver would know. Adrian DeMill, as well as a being a daring driver, was an excellent mechanic — thanks to the United States Marine Corps. If it ran on gasoline or diesel and moved across the surface of the planet, it is likely Adrian could fix it or modify it to work better. He'd modified the Tahoe considerably. It was a desert rat's dream with an enviable list of custom improvements: over-sized radiator, built-in 30-gallon potable water tank, twin oversized gas tanks, industrial model AC unit, ultra-heavy suspension, 6,000-pound capacity Warn winch and a specially modified 350 engine producing 400 horsepower. It was built to take it and built to make it across some of the Southwest's loneliest places. Unless someone was a tire aficionado or climbed inside, though, not many would suspect the Tahoe was anything more than an over-used, played-out refugee from a third-tier used car lot; near perfect camouflage. The Tahoe was Adrian's proudest achievement.

In the front passenger seat sprawled Jack Maxwell, sound asleep. Jack had been Adrian's boss for a while, but now they were partners. Adrian still let Jack call most of the shots. It was easier that way. Jack was better at sorting through and prioritizing the details of a project. Adrian thought of himself as the "action end" of their partnership. Jack decided what needed doing. Adrian did it.

Adrian was a compact man with dark eyes, black hair and pale skin. He was often sun burnt and would probably be a prime candidate for skin cancer later in life should he live long enough, which he really didn't have any expectation of one way or the other. His aversion to sunscreen was based in his own machismo image of himself, which also prevented him from taking off his customary ball cap and adopting something with a wider brim. He was tall enough by a couple of inches to get into the Marines and built like his Tahoe — a deceptively strong interior hidden under a shabby exterior of worn wardrobe and somewhat slovenly personal hygiene. He shaved when he felt like it and seldom combed his hair. His hands were mechanic's hands — never quite clean. Paradoxically, he was meticulous about his teeth and his diet. Adrian loved good food.

On a personal level, Adrian didn't like Jack very much, but on a personal level, Adrian didn't like anyone very much. His picture might have been beside "misanthrope" in the dictionary. And right at that moment in Adrian's custom-built Tahoe, the guy in the passenger's seat was snoring.

Jack had demonstrated this talent numerous times during their relationship. Adrian disliked him a bit more each time. In thoughts keeping cadence with Jack's snores, Adrian — convinced that Abel had snored, and Cain was completely justified — often considered killing the snorer.

This was not an idle thought for Adrian DeMill. He'd killed people before. In the early going in Iraq, the Marine Corps took his wrenches away and made him a rifle-bearer. Lighting up the enemy had become his sole pleasure and reason for being. However, when he rotated home and mustered out — he'd had some issues with discipline and authority and the Corps wouldn't let him re-enlist — his misanthropia wouldn't let him hold a mechanic's job for long and there wasn't much market for his non-mechanic skills in the States. There was a market in Mexico, though. The border drug trade needed folks like Adrian to "keep the mules honest," as his employer was fond of saying.

So, he found a job on the cusp between Old and New Mexico and met Jack Maxwell, a cadre boss in the employment of the same group as Adrian. Eventually, Jack became Adrian's immediate supervisor and Adrian became Jack's *segundo*, read "enforcer."

Jack was tall, thin and blonde. All of the caution Adrian did not display about the sun, Jack piled on top of his own. SPF 50 was his best friend and he never went anywhere without a wide-brimmed Stetson or, in more active mode, a Foreign Legion-type hat with a reflective skirt that covered his ears and the back of his neck.

Jack and Adrian were "on sabbatical" from the drug trade. The border business had gotten hot, and, as gringos, the two of them stuck out like sore thumbs. The big boss sent them north for a little time off, which Jack and Adrian both understood was better than other alternatives used by their employer when someone became a small liability. It was good to know they were of enough value to be considered less than purely disposable.

The trouble was that income dropped to nil, and neither Jack nor Adrian was a good saver. A rainy day had arrived, and neither had an umbrella. So, they — Adrian, actually — robbed a few 7-Elevens to get by, and Jack put his feelers out for a "real" job.

They found one, which is why they are parked under a canyon wall four miles from where Opal, Helen and Ross are camped at Cottonwood Campground in western Colorado. Their mission, which they have accepted, is to kidnap and hold for ransom Opal Skladany.

How Jack knows about Opal or that her dad and her mom are both worth several millions is unclear to Adrian. Jack isn't sharing anything Adrian doesn't have to know; just a vague reference to "someone I used to know in high school," whom Adrian has come to think of as The Contact. Adrian isn't concerned about historic details. Payday is coming, payday with individual shares in the six-figure range. The number five-hundred thousand has been bandied about. As his share. He could retire from the bad guy business — though he knew he would miss the excitement — go home to Cali, open a custom desert rig shop in Bakersfield and launder that half a mil back into the economy over the course of 20 years and never have to shoot at anyone again. Or get shot at.

That was Adrian's plan, anyway. He wasn't sure what Jack would do, but the thought had occurred to him that this was a big desert, and if he had two shares, the laundering could last 30 years, and he would have a better lifestyle. Not that he was committed to that course of action, but it was there to consider.

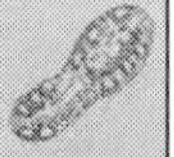

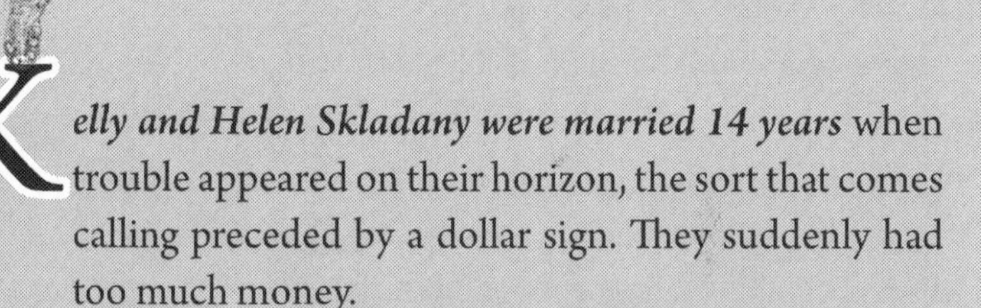

Chapter Five: Running From Glaciers

Kelly and Helen Skladany were married 14 years when trouble appeared on their horizon, the sort that comes calling preceded by a dollar sign. They suddenly had too much money.

Kelly was one of the founders of iTrac, an Internet startup specializing in web-based information management that offered stock options to its employees. When it went public — well, the IPO was a success. The Skladany household went from lower middle class income to upper class income in about a month. Their marriage did not survive the impact. Now that they could afford about anything they wanted, they discovered that they didn't want the same things. At least, Kelly didn't.

If Joe Skladany had been privy to his son's actions at that point — as Helen slowly became and Sabrina was from the first — he would not have been so tickled about Opal's actions at this point, but one-sided reporting is a hallmark of family meltdowns. Joe hadn't gotten to hear what Helen had to say about any of this except that Helen had told his son she wanted a divorce. Kelly was not about to reveal the details to his dad, because he knew his old-fashioned old man would never understand.

It was not an amicable divorce. The aggrieved party (Helen) became unreasonable about what was hers (everything) and what was his (not a single, damned dime), and the ensuing fight enriched a couple of Seattle lawyers but didn't really change the outcome much. Helen and Kelly split the new fortune (less legal fees) and custody of Opal. Helen got the house in Seattle. Kelly built a new place at Copalis Beach. The nature of child exchange was that whosever turn it was would take the Bremerton/Seattle ferry to the other side, where Opal would be waiting with Helen in Seattle or Kelly in Bremerton.

School was a bit disjointed for Opal, because she went to two. But she liked that, as it gave her cause to be somewhat mysterious and dramatic in her comings and goings. If there was a way thirteen-year-old Opal liked to be, it was mysterious and dramatic. It caused her teachers to be concerned at first, but Opal was never "behind" because of this arrangement. In fact, she was often "ahead" of her classmates, because Opal was a genius.

This was apparent to her parents, a couple of her grandparents (Joe and Helen's mother, Maggie), many of her teachers and a few of her friends. The rest of the world did not notice, partly because genius is not a physical trait easily seen, and partly because Opal hadn't yet figured out she was a genius, or what it meant to be one.

One of the things Opal did know about herself was that she loved to run. Not only that, she was good at it. She started running regularly at about the same time her folks began not getting along, and, yes, one had something to do with the other. It was the only time she could spend with her dad that wasn't marred by the recrimination of her mother.

In the early days of alienation, an icy presence slipped into any room that Kelly and Helen shared. Even in her innocence, Opal could feel it, and it chilled her to the bone. Something told her that the glacier thing (which is how she thought of it) was slowly taking her dad farther and farther away from her mom, who seemed to be standing on a immovable rock, watching and unwilling to do anything but observe.

She could feel the glacier thing when she was alone with her mother, but when she went running with her dad, it fell behind her, as if she could run away from it. She sometimes wondered if her dad was also able to run away from it, and that was why he ran. But she never asked him.

Her dad was a recreation and fitness runner. For Opal, running with her dad was the best. It was their secret joy, and even Helen's glacier thing couldn't overcome it.

Opal feared that eventually the glacier thing would calve and her dad would be taken out to sea on an iceberg, which is what happened, sort of. He'd then washed up at Capolis Beach, where he seemed to Opal somewhat marooned and lonely, even when Sabrina was around. That's the kind of genius that Opal was.

In a year, she could outrun her dad, but she tried not to. Instead, she started running on her own and now she was on two middle-school cross-country teams; one in Hoquiam and the other in Seattle. She was good enough that neither coach was picky about her irregular presence. In fact, she already held records for her age in both King and Grays Harbor Counties.

In the end, the quasi-chance meeting with Sabrina had been on a run. Sabrina was introduced as one of her dad's coworkers, which she was, and a casual acquaintance, which she wasn't. Then they all went running together, which is when Opal found out that Sabrina was funny and fun, and also that she could keep up.

Chapter Six: Navigation

All Adrian knew about The Contact was that he had a funny voice. He sometimes vaguely heard it when Jack got a call on his cell phone, and the voice was sort of squeaky. But he never got to listen long, as Jack always made his "this is private" face and turned away. The Contact was feeding Jack information about the person they were going to kidnap.

Four days ago, they left New Mexico on Interstate 25, herding the Tahoe into Colorado. North of Pueblo, they turned west on Highway 50 and crossed the Rockies to Montrose. After a three nights in a motel, Jack got a phone call in the morning and they then drove northwest through Delta. Shortly after that, they turned on a secondary road that crossed the Gunnison River. With Jack navigating using a GPS, they found their way to the canyon they waited in now.

Adrian wasn't up to speed on the digital age. He could never quite figure all that stuff out, but Jack had it dialed. In fact, Jack never left home without his gadgets, which made Adrian feel somewhat superior, for he was good with map and compass and had an inner homing beacon that was always on. Once he had been to a place, he could always find his way back there.

There were no exceptions to this that he knew of. One of his earliest memories was of a trip in a car with his mother from where they lived in San Clemente up a country road in the hills near town, where they had encountered a gate. His mom got out of the car and talked into a box for quite a while until the gate magically opened. Then they drove up a hill to a huge house, where she parked the car in the shade of a big oak tree and told young Adrian that if he left the car he would get a beating.

She was gone for what seemed like forever but when she came back, she seemed happier than young Adrian had ever seen her. She waved a piece of paper at him and said something it took him a long time to understand. "We're on Easy Street now, kiddo."

They didn't even go back to the place they were staying in San Clemente, and Adrian never saw the man they had been living with again, which he thought was good, because he wasn't very nice to Adrian or his mom. That was when they moved to Bakersfield.

Adrian thought about that ride many times. Almost 20 years later, when he got out of the Marine Corps, he drove back to the little house they had lived in with the not-so-nice guy near the beach in San Clemente and retraced the route his mom had taken to the big gate. On the gate in wrought iron was his own last name — DeMill. This intrigued him. He got out and pushed the button on the talking box. A woman's voice answered, "May I help you?"

"My name is Adrian DeMill," he said, "and my mom brought me here when I was three. Do you know me?"

There was a long pause. Adrian then heard a noise above his head. He looked up to see a camera on top of one of the gateposts pointed directly at him. The sound was that of the telephoto lens focusing on him. He looked directly into the lens.

"I'm afraid you must have the wrong place," the box said.

"No," Adrian said. "This is the place. I never forget a place I've been to."

"I can't help you, young man," the box said, and it made a noise that told Adrian it had been switched off. The camera swiveled away. Ninety seconds later, a black Suburban with shaded windows came down the driveway and stopped inside the gate. Nobody got out. Adrian said, mostly to himself, "I can take a hint," and drove slowly back down the road to San Clemente. He decided then that someday he would use his Marine-gained skills to have a look around inside that gate.

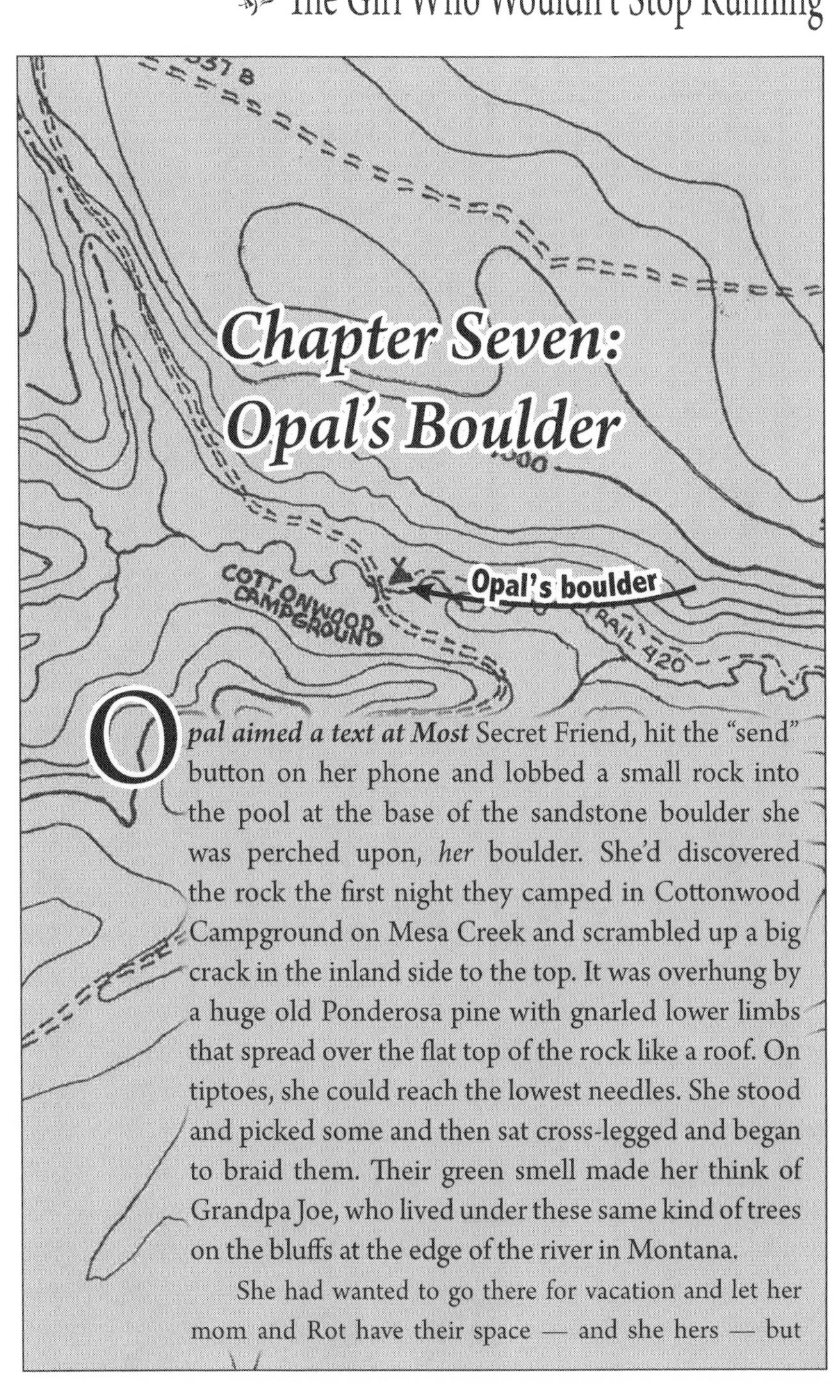

Chapter Seven: Opal's Boulder

Opal aimed a text at Most Secret Friend, hit the "send" button on her phone and lobbed a small rock into the pool at the base of the sandstone boulder she was perched upon, *her* boulder. She'd discovered the rock the first night they camped in Cottonwood Campground on Mesa Creek and scrambled up a big crack in the inland side to the top. It was overhung by a huge old Ponderosa pine with gnarled lower limbs that spread over the flat top of the rock like a roof. On tiptoes, she could reach the lowest needles. She stood and picked some and then sat cross-legged and began to braid them. Their green smell made her think of Grandpa Joe, who lived under these same kind of trees on the bluffs at the edge of the river in Montana.

She had wanted to go there for vacation and let her mom and Rot have their space — and she hers — but

Helen insisted that she come with them. All the way up the Columbia to the Snake, then up the Snake to Lewiston, up the Clearwater and Lochsa and over the top of the Bitterroots, she held out in the back seat, texting Most Secret Friend when and where there was cell reception, and trying to be as properly miserable as she could. Even so, scenes flowing by called out to her. She had never seen such places as they were visiting, and in spite of her best intentions to have no fun at all, she was drawn out again and again. She could feel her surliness evaporate in off-the-highway campsites they searched out most nights, pulled out of her by golden-red flames and wood smoke and the deep well of darkness that surrounded them when the Coleman lantern was turned off.

Camped in an open sage meadow in the Stanley Basin, she caught herself listening to Ross — umm, Rot —name the stars, and willed herself to stay awake far into the night, staring through the gauzy top of the tent at the heavens. As the sky rotated slowly above her, she grudgingly admitted to herself that Rot knew a lot of cool things. For a creep, anyway.

Now, they were encamped in the most beautiful place she had ever been. It was full of foreign, delicately painted cliffs and boulders and oddly delicious smells and cacti and big dragon flies that would be knocked out of the sky by the weather in Washington. She loved this place. It was so secret that even Most Secret Friend might not be able to find her here — although Opal was pretty sure MSF could. MSF was one of the smartest people Opal knew. And she was totally able to keep a secret.

Most Secret Friend and Opal had, upon agreeing to be each other's most secret friend, also agreed that texting was the best way to correspond, though occasional voice contact was OK in emergencies. They further agreed not to tell anyone about their private communications, especially boys. Even when MSF and Opal saw each other, MSF never did or said anything that might let the world in on their confidential conversations. Opal tested MSF once by alluding to their secret in person, just to see what MSF would do. Opal got such an expression from MSF that she was embarrassed to have tried and convinced MSF would never breach their agreement.

On this journey, Opal had discovered that when she put a text into her phone, the phone would sometimes ask "Would you like to deliver this message when there is service?" This was particularly true since they had camped at Cottonwood. In this case, she would key the "yes" button and sometime later, often even if she didn't move, the phone would make its "I just sent a text message" sound. This added more appeal to the place, that it could and would send out messages when *it* was ready. When she was a grownup, she decided, she was going to come here to live. She would build a little house out of red and yellow rocks and come to her boulder every day and write in a notebook about life.

Opal had come to her boulder after the last bout with her mother. She didn't want to go hiking with Rot she had affirmed, but as she sat on her big chunk of sandstone, she knew that was a big, fat lie. She *did* want to go down the canyon — on Mesa Creek Trail #420, said the sign at the campground. She wanted to see more and more of this heavenly place. Even the hard parts.

She looked down the canyon. In the evening distance, expanses of uninhabited stone stretched in inverted arcs up from the creek, growing drier and hotter with each foot of distance from the water. She wanted to scramble up to the bottom of the cliffs and look into each of the dark slots that came into the canyon from all sides. Away down the valley, she could see a collection of green, and she knew it was an oasis even better than the one they were camped in.

Yes, she wished to go there.

Rot was going to hike there tomorrow morning first thing, but she couldn't let herself like him enough to go along. Couldn't. Shouldn't. Wouldn't. Even though she bet he could tell her the names of things along the way, and maybe even make her laugh with his goofy "scientific" names for things.

Pinus tallus, he called the ponderosas. *Pinus shortus* were the piñons. *Pinus pricklius* were the junipers. A prickly pear was *Ouchus holycowus.* Sagebrush was *smellumus goodus.* He was so sincerely sure of it all that even Opal, the greatest Rot hater of all time, privately giggled about it. She knew that he knew these weren't real names, that he was a lot smarter than that, and it was his smarts that let him make up these names so adroitly and remember them so well.

Opal knew that Rot really knew all sorts of things, but maybe the thing he knew best was how to be funny. Opal's mom was always laughing when Rot was around. Even in the early days of her loathing, Opal had joined her surreptitiously; always making sure that neither of the adults knew she was amused.

Opal sat on her rock and struggled with her dilemna. If she said she wanted to go with Rot, she was betraying her mission to drive him out of their lives and to never let anyone replace her dad. If she didn't say she wanted to go, she would lose her one chance in maybe a million years to walk down that canyon and into that oasis away out at the edge of sight. Day after tomorrow, they would put everything back in the Explorer and begin back north. In a few short days, she would be back in rainy, green Seattle, sitting in Whitman Middle School being bored out of her skull learning things she already knew.

Sitting cross-legged in the midst of her dilemma, braiding pungent, green *Pinus tallus* needles into a plait, she heard footsteps — her mother's, she knew — and she guessed that Helen had come to plead once more for her to go with Rot. *Please,* she prayed, *let her say the right thing the right way.*

"Opal?" her mother called. "Are you up there?"

"Yes." She tried to sound surly.

"Opal," her mother said, very assertively and very kindly, and Opal's ears perked up.

Maybe, she thought. *Maybe we can make this work.*

"Day after tomorrow," Helen continued, "you and Ross and I are going to pack up and leave here. In a few days, you will be back at school in Seattle and then Hoquiam. You may never in your life get back to this spot, because God only knows what life has in store. I don't care if you say a single word to Ross all day. Frankly, neither does he. He's a man, not a child, and your obstinacy neither makes him feel better nor worse about himself — or you."

Fearing that Opal might not understand this, Helen paused. But Opal did understand, and she was surprised that she did. What her mother was saying was that no matter what she did, Rot was part of the picture. She wasn't going to scare him off or drive him away with her loathing. Rot didn't care what she thought of him. Not one iota. And something in her mother's voice told her that Helen didn't care either.

She searched her referential data and tried to put all this in perspective. In her experience, even her dad cared what she thought of him and sometimes modified his behavior to affect that. She'd seen him do it. But this guy Rot didn't give a — she secretly thought the word *damn,* completely forbidden but highly appropriate — *darn* whether she liked him or not.

So it didn't matter. She could loathe him *and* go hiking with him. *And* laugh at some (but not all) of his jokes. She could, in this case, give up and let things be as they were. If they were going to be as they were, she got to go hiking without betraying anything.

Her phone made the "You just got a text" sound. She flipped it open and the message from Most Secret Friend read, "If you want to go, you should."

"Anyway, Opal," Helen continued, "this is your last chance to see as much of this place as you can. I would suggest that you get down off that rock and get ready to go."

Much to Helen's surprise, a few minutes later, Opal did exactly that.

Helen would rue that conversation. It would replay in her head for days and weeks to come, and she would try each time it played to decide if she was to blame for what happened at the edge of that green spot at the edge of sight away down the canyon.

She wasn't.

Chapter Eight: An American Oasis

In the Tahoe parked against a canyon wall above Mesa Creek, Jack turned to his right and pulled his left leg up into the seat. His snoring cadence changed, and Adrian decided it was time to take a little walk. "One must be patient," he told himself, mimicking a fifth-grade teacher who had taunted him long ago with that mantra as he sat looking out at the other kids at recess; on detention once again for displaying his inabilities in book learning.

Sometimes he wondered if Mrs. French was still alive, and what kids she had picked on after he got out of her class. It was plain she didn't like him like she did the others. He almost never went to recess, he thought probably because he didn't "smell like money," as one of his step-dads often said with disdain when talking about folks more well off.

"I'm gonna smell like money soon," he thought.

He pulled on his bill cap and got out of the Tahoe as quietly as he could. It was almost cool in the shadows of his side canyon. Evening was coming on. At 6,500 feet, the desert was tolerable at this time of year, and he was glad for the altitude. He hiked down the side canyon to where it began to drop steeply into Mesa Creek and several hundred yards later walked out into the larger canyon and the lowering rays of the sun. On some semblance of a trail, he scrambled another quarter mile and 300 vertical feet down a talus alluvia to Mesa Creek

Adrian had seen his share of deserts, but he was taken with this place. Not as spectacular as the Grand Canyon or the Green River, it was still hauntingly beautiful; red and yellow sandstone piled in huge layers one atop the other rising toward the crown of the plateau. Up canyon, he could see the rim of the highland — 9,000 feet his Colorado atlas told him. The face of the rimrock was studded with dark green dots he knew to be piñon pine and topped with a fringe of taller trees, Ponderosas.

The creek here was not much of a stream at this time of year, just a series of separate and elongated pools, but there still remained a respectable amount of water feeding willows, dogwood and osiers, cottonwood and poplars, as well as an occasional pocket of juniper, ponderosa and anomalous Douglas firs. He turned upstream along a well-worn trail marked with cairns and blazes on available trees and intuited that this trail was where they would encounter the kid they were going to take. A few minutes later, he was surprised to come to an ascending series of ancient beaver ponds. This was the explanation for the water down lower, he decided, a slow-release reservoir. In the sedgey areas behind the old dams grew a lush mixture of cattails, grasses, forbs, shrubs and mosses. Adrian wondered if fish hid in the pools that remained unsilted.

He continued upstream looking for a satisfactory place for an ambush before he settled on a spot at the upper end of a stretch of trail where it meandered through a boulder field for several hundred yards. It seemed perfect for what he had in mind, a narrow opening between two huge chunks of sandstone that had actually been one piece a thousand years before when it fell from the wall above.

Adrian knew it would be up to him to take the girl. Jack was not an action person. He was fit enough to get in and out of the canyon, need be, but neither an athlete nor physically assertive. A thirteen-year-old might just get away from him. Once the girl was immobilized, Jack could watch her, but Adrian knew it was up to him to capture and subdue her. He envisioned what would happen if certain elements were present and practiced certain moves until settling on a scenario he thought would work.

He turned back downstream and stopped at the ponds to sit on a boulder beside the trail and contemplate this American oasis. In all of his time in the deserts of southern Arizona and New Mexico, he'd never seen anything so beautiful as this place was this evening. This was the kind of place that could almost make him forget that he hated nearly everyone and they hated him.

At first he thought of the place as being very quiet, but as he sat still, it began to come to life around him. First one bird and then others began to chirp and twitter and flit around the ponds. A bright yellow number — *What the heck* is *that,* he wondered — crossed in front of him in connected swoops and disappeared into thick juniper. Cicadas began to hiss out their extended song. Soon, the whole place seemed alive.

In his peripheral vision, something big moved, and his reflexes put the 9 mm pistol under his arm into his hand as quickly as any old-time gunfighter might have drawn. He found he had pulled his weapon on a huge mule deer buck that was just as surprised to see him as he was it. After two heartbeats, one for Adrian and one for the deer, the buck clattered up the canyon wall on some trail too slight for Adrian to see and then out of sight into a crack in the sandstone rim.

Adrian cast a sigh of relief, put his pistol away and turned back to the ponds. The place had gone still. No birds. No cicadas. He sat down again. The last of the sun was warm on his back. Something moved in one of the pools. A cicada began to whirr. A bird chirped in one of the clumps of cattails. A tiny brown something-or-other — *I* gotta *get me a bird book,* Adrian thought — flitted up the canyon and another bird began to sing in one of the cottonwoods.

Adrian sat on his rock for a long time, until the sun was nearly gone and the air began to cool. Then, although he really didn't care to ruin his day by waking up his partner, he got up and hiked back to the Tahoe.

When he got there, Jack was awake. *Dammit, anyway,* Adrian thought. He pulled a wall tent out of the back and began to set camp. Somebody had to do it.

Chapter Nine: Most Secret Friend

J*ust before she went to sleep,* Opal heard the "I just sent a text message" sound from her phone, which made her smile. A few minutes before, she had punched in a cryptic text. "Tomorrow morning at dawn, Mesa Creek Trail #420 to the oasis." She wondered briefly if MSF could figure out where she was, and then she nodded off.

Miles away, a phone made the "You just got a text message" sound, and Most Secret Friend woke from a fitful drowse and looked at the text. Fifteen minutes later, MSF was in a 24-hour truck stop café with free wireless and a laptop on the table. Google Earth was running and onscreen was an image of the Uncompahgre Plateau from 30,000 feet. MSF opened a browser, and keyed "Mesa Creek Trail #420, Uncompahgre" into the search window and pulled up an image from a Colorado hiking club site.

There it was, stretching from Cottonwood Campground to the Gunnison and finally a trailhead on Highway 50. Most Secret Friend copied the coordinates of the upper trailhead, pasted them into Google Earth and zoomed down to about a half-mile from the surface. And smiled. This was going to work after all. After all of the sketchy, flakey, seat-of-your pants stuff of the past few days, Jack and his buddy Alan or Andrew or whatever his name was were just a bit more than a mile from Opal's oasis. By some strokes of good fortune and some stellar guessing on the part of MSF, this was coming together.

Most Secret Friend keyed a text into their phone, "In the morning. More to follow." MSF hit "send," and drove home through a sudden rainstorm.

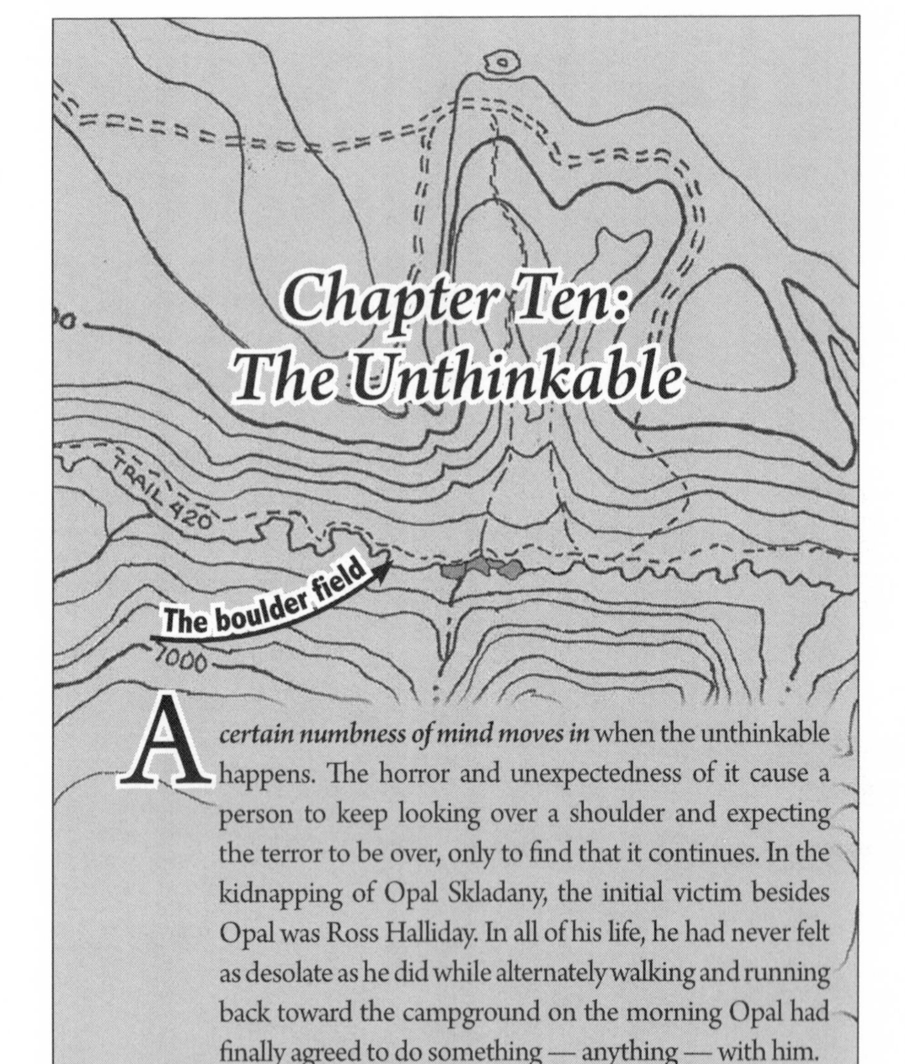

Chapter Ten: The Unthinkable

A *certain numbness of mind moves in* when the unthinkable happens. The horror and unexpectedness of it cause a person to keep looking over a shoulder and expecting the terror to be over, only to find that it continues. In the kidnapping of Opal Skladany, the initial victim besides Opal was Ross Halliday. In all of his life, he had never felt as desolate as he did while alternately walking and running back toward the campground on the morning Opal had finally agreed to do something — anything — with him.

Clutched in his hand was a large ziplock bag, and in the bag was a single piece of paper inscribed on both sides with a nightmare in block letters written with a felt-tip pen.

"Opal is safe for exactly 48 hours," was the first thing Ross saw through the plastic, "unless law enforcement is called. If law enforcement is involved, Opal will be killed."

The rest of the message read, "Bring a backpack containing $2,000,000 in cash to the exact spot this was found at exactly 4 pm tomorrow. Bring 20s, 50s and 100s that are used and clean. If this deadline is missed or the money is marked, Opal will be killed.

"Leave the spot completely after leaving the money. If anyone is detected within three miles at any time one hour after the money is left, Opal will be killed.

"Opal will be released exactly 24 hours after the money is delivered. If any attempt is made to rescue her, she will be killed."

The bag was laying in the trail between the two halves of the broken boulder when he went back to see what had distracted Opal this time. She had been dawdling since they left camp, stopping to take pictures and poke into this and that and then catching up. After the first few times, he let it be. He wanted her to enjoy this day as much as possible and it appeared that she was. She was an independent soul, Opal was, and summers in Montana at her grandpa's place had made her comfortable in the wild. Joe Skladany was famous for letting his grandkids run amok. Ringleader Opal and her gang of cousins knew where the fences on Joe's place were, how to climb through them and how to get home before sunset.

Opal's final acceptance of Ross' invitation to hike had pleased him greatly. He nearly assumed he had won her over, but backed away from that when it occurred to him that a battle was not a war and no peace treaty had been signed. She presented herself for breakfast as agreed — long before the sun was up — pink backpack and all, but still with a certain hint of disgust that they were in the same hemisphere. As he cooked to the light of the Coleman lantern, he asked her a question.

"Are you willing to allow me leadership of this little expedition, Opal?"

"What do you mean, 'leadership?' " Suspicion dripped from every one of the first five words she had spoken to him in two days.

"We're going into a hard place, one that can hurt or kill you if you aren't careful, and particularly if you don't know what you're doing."

"So?"

Her tone almost made him say, "Forget it. With that attitude, you can't come." But not quite. He took a breath and looked out to the west, where the last holdout stars were giving way to the coming day.

"So, this," he said gently. "As long as we're out, I'm the boss. If I say we need to do something, there's no argument."

Opal slumped a little, and looked disgusted.

"Yes or no?" Ross turned from dishing up a couple of plates of scrambled eggs and potatoes, which on earlier occasions, Opal might have refused. But Opal remembered that he didn't give a — *darn* — about what she thought of him. And she was starving.

"OK," she said.

"Good." He set a steaming plate in front her and sat down with his. "That doesn't mean you don't have any say, Opal. I'm open to a suggestion any time. Do you have lots of water?"

"Three liters," she said.

"Extra food?"

"Yes." She intimated by the tone of her answer that he was an idiot and saw a flash in his eye. His jaw muscles tighten. Something said, *Opal, if you really want to go, back off.*

"I'm ready," she volunteered.

Ross smiled. "OK. Good. Let's eat."

Helen joined them as they finished their breakfast and was grateful to see them eating together.

At 5:30 Mountain time, Opal's phone had given her a wakeup greeting, a message from MSF: "Send me a text when you wake up." Opal replied, "Awake. Leaving after breakfast." A few minutes later she was at the picnic table and heard the familiar confirmation noise. Rot had looked up from cooking and frowned but said nothing. When he turned back to the stove, Opal set her phone to vibrate.

Ten minutes later, the arrival of a text message on Jack's phone caused Adrian to poke the other man. Adrian, who had been awake since 4, had what he needed in order and was about to wake Jack anyway. It seemed to him time to get moving. Jack awoke with a start, and Adrian pointed at his phone. Jack looked at the text.

"Not more than ninety minutes," he said. Jack made quick preparations and they began for Mesa Creek and the boulder field. It was 5:50 and just light enough to see without head lamps.

At 6:00, Ross and Opal shouldered their packs and began. The sun would be up in another hour. Helen waved them goodbye, cast a sigh of relief and after a moment decided it was really too nice a morning to go back to bed.

Over an hour later, Ross and Opal finally reached the boulder field. Adrian had been watching for half an hour from a spot above the field in a little cove in the canyon wall, examining the pattern of the two of them; the man hiking slowly but steadily and Opal falling behind and catching up. If he could catch the girl in the falling behind stage, it would be perfect. They could leave the man out of it completely, no need for him to even see Adrian or Jack, although they would leave the ski masks on in any case until Opal was secured. And that is how it happened.

Opal was dragging behind a hundred yards when Ross walked through the gap in the broken-in-half boulder. When Opal reached the spot, Adrian stepped out from hiding and wrapped a hand around her mouth to keep her from crying out. A moment later, her mouth was duct-taped shut and Adrian had her over his shoulder, climbing to a spot he had picked the day before, making sure he stayed on rock and left no tracks. Jack dropped the baggie with the note from the top of the broken boulder. It was done in less than 10 seconds.

Ross stopped to wait at the downstream edge of the boulder field, 150 yards from the broken-in-half rock. When Opal failed to show up in what he thought was a reasonable time, he called, "C'mon, Opal. Let's go."

There are certain kinds of silence, and the one hanging over that boulder field that morning suddenly seemed to Ross to be too complete. No birds sang. Nothing moved.

"Opal?" Ross shouted a little louder.

One minute later, Ross, who was half angry and half worried, found the baggie in the middle of the trail. With wooden fingers, he picked it up and read the first page. He looked for Opal's tracks overlaying his own, but they disappeared just before the trail entered into the split in the boulder. There was not a sign of any others. None.

"Opal!" It was a full-volume cry this time. In the canyon above, Sara Cafferty looked up from her standing morning date with geology and frowned.

About an hour later and hundreds of miles to the north, the lead dog began into a long and troublesome dream. It was, as these sorts of dreams always are, in living color and eminently memorable, down to the last detail.

Chapter Eleven: A Telling Dream

Archer had this dream on the morning of Sara's "Today," three mornings after he had flown Skladany, Turnbull, Sevlakovs, et. al. into the back country for a little smoke jumping. This was supposed to be the beginning of some well-earned days off for all of them. The dream would preclude that. In spite of its beauty and memorability, this was not the kind of dream that Archer liked to have. It was the kind of dream his mother called The Telling Dreams.

"This dream is telling you something," she said to him when he was young and dared to share one with her. "You will probably have more. You will learn to pay them attention."

She was not completely happy to tell him that, but neither was she filled with sorrow. Silvie MacClehan knew about Telling Dreams. She had them herself, and hers brought both kinds of news — good and bad — and an occasional warning. She was, however, concerned that Archer understand the responsibility that went with the dreaming.

Silvie's muse was a woman she'd never met but knew nonetheless — Angela Tommason, her father's adoptive mother. Angela died a month after Silvie was born in the log house above Willow Creek without ever seeing Silvie.

When Silvie was 13, Angela came to her in the night and brought her a book. She put it in Silvie's lap and motioned her to open it. When Silvie split the pages, she found herself looking into a glorious place full of all shapes and colors of folk wearing incredible costumes and strange clothing and sometimes nothing at all. She wanted nothing more than to jump into this place and find out as much as she could about the people, but the old woman stopped her by taking the book out of her lap and closing it. She turned it so Silvie could see the spine. Laid down the back of the book was the image of a tree branch etched in gold. And Silvie awoke.

She took this first Telling Dream to her mother, Irene Skaar Tommason. Irene was Norwegian by birth, Presbyterian by calling and a polytheistic animist by acquisition. As a young, blonde missionary called to the reservation at Yakima, she met and came to love a man whose mother was Nez Perce and father was Lakota Sioux. His names were Alfred Tommason in the white world of his adoptive parents and Five Bears in the native world.

Irene's marriage to Alfred, which she called him all the rest of her life except on certain important and intimate occasions, opened her eyes and mind to a reality alternative to the one she was called into. She came to accept that there were many ways to relate to the Spirit, and that the Spirit spoke in many ways; ways she could sometimes comprehend and sometimes could not. It always pleased Irene when she understood. When Silvie told her dream, Irene was pleased to rise out of her chair by the window and walk to the rough-hewn bookcase that took up the entire interior wall of the big main room of the house. She reached definitively for a book, hooked the top of it with a finger and tipped it out of the case. She opened it and peered inside as Silvie watched and wondered if her mother was seeing the people she had seen.

When Irene brought the book to Silvie, she also brought an enigmatic smile Silvie had never seen. It made her look very wise, Silvie thought, and old. No. Not old, but ancient; like the rocks that made up the east end of the meadow behind the barn — timeless. Irene handed the book to Silvie, and Silvie turned the spine so she could read it.

In gold type, the title stood: *The Golden Bough.*

Ten years later, on a fine June day in Bozeman, Silver Dawn Tommason — soon to be MacClehan — accepted her bachelor's degree in cultural anthropology from Montana State University. She did not necessarily agree upon completion of her degree with Fraser's view of the cultures of the world. He was a somewhat chauvinist male member in good standing of the Victorian British Empire. She was a half native, half white Western American, but she was grateful to him nonetheless. She also knew the power of The Telling Dreams, and her counsel to her son, ten years after that, was that he should honor them and follow their leading.

Archer was willing to do so, but he would find that his telling dreams sometimes — but not always — led him into places he might otherwise not wish to go; dangerous places, unpleasant places, places where lives were on the line, including his own. He had come to accept them, but he did not always see them as blessings. He did not necessarily like having these dreams.

But, he was having one, and even as he was dreaming, part of him knew he would go into it. There was no other way. If he didn't chase the dream, it would chase him.

As nearly always in the dream, he was a boy and Five Bears was instructing him in the use of the bow and arrow. Archer could feel the old man's hand on his shoulder, and knew from experience he couldn't turn to look at him. They were hunting Archer knew not for what; sitting motionless and waiting for some prey to approach.

It was hot, even in the shade of a huge Ponderosa pine. It was late in the day. The tree's shadow fell across Archer sitting very still in a patch of rabbit brush near the bottom of a canyon with sandstone walls. Archer was hung with brush and his face was streaked with gray soot.

"Watch the sky," Five Bears said.

Two dark shapes appeared in the south, and Archer recognized them as birds rowing their way through the air toward him. He recognized them first as very large and then as vultures. The vultures moved into a circling pattern above his hiding spot. He worried they might see him, even as he knew they could not see Five Bears.

"Look right," the old man said. As he swiveled his head, an outsized coral snake slithered into view. Following it intently, oblivious to the venomous nature of the reptile, came a small person, a young girl — Opal Skladany! The vultures circled down and one landed beside the snake. The other swooped in behind the girl, snatched her off the ground and flew into a crack in the canyon wall. Archer began to rise and follow, but the old man hissed, "Not yet, or they will kill her." The snake coiled and abruptly disappeared.

At that moment, Opal came running out of the side canyon the vulture had taken her into. The other vulture rose from where it had landed near the snake and soon was hot on her heels.

"Now!" said Five Bears. "Shoot!"

He threw himself to standing position and sighted on the vulture. He released, and saw that his arrow was pulling a cord, which entangled the vulture's feet and legs. The line went taut and the bird crashed to the ground. The vulture struggled against the cord wrapped about its legs and then suddenly went limp.

The shadow of the other bird came across Archer from behind. He reached for another arrow, but his quiver was empty. The huge bird turned, closing fast. Archer looked for a club or a rock, but the only object nearby was his backpack. He picked up the pack and slung it at the oncoming bird. The vulture snagged it out of the air and made a swooping turn into the side canyon where it had disappeared earlier with Opal, all the while emitting a high-pitched human laugh.

The vulture with the entangled feet seemed to be melting into the rock. Beyond it, Opal ran pell mell down the canyon. In front of Opal, the coral snake began to appear and disappear, as if switching on and off, finally leading Opal abruptly up the canyon wall and out of sight over the rim. Archer began after them, but a hand on his shoulder held him back.

He tried to pull away. Five Bears held on. "Look west."

Archer looked toward the setting sun and saw against the light a small shape rising and falling rhythmically in a running cadence. It came closer and soon he recognized it as human, and then as a woman; a small woman with red hair and fair skin. Sara! Sweat was streaming off of her and she waved and smiled as she went by. His heart leapt in his chest.

As he watched her chase after Opal and the snake, the thought of her confronting the snake alone terrified Archer. Again, he tried to run, and again, Five Bears stopped him.

"Running Woman is stronger than the snake and can run longer than the little one," Five Bears said. "She and the little one will both stop running."

Then something remarkable happened, as if the dream wasn't remarkable enough. Five Bears pulled Archer around to face him, and for one of the very few times in any of the dreams, Archer saw his face. He wasn't the old man Archer expected, but a native man in his prime with long dark hair held back from his face by a leather thong and dressed in not much, a tanned leather breech clout and tall moccasins — desert attire. He wore no paint or decorations of any sort, no headband, no leggings. He was stocky and well-muscled, and he carried a short hunting bow and a quiver of arrows. A stone blade with an antler handle hung on a rawhide cord around his waist.

For a long moment, Five Bears looked deep into Archer and Archer felt his soul stirring. Old, dark feelings and memories rose into his throat like bile. Five Bears pointed and Archer looked to see Sara disappear over the rim. He felt his heart shattering.

The native man said, "To catch Running Woman, you must stop running. A broken heart does not mend in the dark."

A***rcher abruptly awoke looking at*** the bedroom ceiling in his house on Short Creek Road, a long way from the desert he had been dreaming of.

The phone was ringing, and he knew by the light streaming in the window that he had slept far past his usual time. He also knew before he answered that the caller was Joe Skladany.

Chapter Twelve: Upon Waking

J***oe's anguished voice was nearly unrecognizable.*** "AJ, someone's taken Opal."

Archer was still trying to push his dream out of the way, and this seemed a continuation. "Vultures," he said.

"Goddam hyenas! Jackals!" Joe's rage tore out of him, and a long string of invectives followed. Finally, he came to the end of that and got quiet. "AJ, I don't know what to do, but I gotta do something. She was out hiking with her step-father, or whatever he is, and someone took her right out from under his nose — stupid, blind, bumbling fool. Never would have happened if it had been Kelly, I tell you."

Archer took a deep breath and pushed it against his diaphragm.

"AJ? You there? I need some help. They're down in Colorado. I need to get down there. Will you fly me down?"

Archer knew this was his entrée into the reality of the dream. He couldn't say "No," but he wanted to slow things down a bit. "OK, Joe. Steady down. There's work to do," he said. "First of all, Opal's going to be OK."

"How do you *know* that? How can you know?"

"I just know. So you relax a little and let me think about what I need to do. Yes. I'll fly you. But there are some folks we want to take with us, and I need to file a flight plan. Can you give me some details about the place where she was taken?"

"It's on the Uncompahgre Plateau. They're staying at a campground called Cottonwood. The trail starts at the campground and runs down a canyon — Mesa Creek Canyon. The bastards took her and left a note. They want two million — cash. By tomorrow! Where in the hell is anyone going to get that?

"Has anyone called the FBI?"

"The note said if we call the police, they'll kill her. Kill her! Sons-of-bitches!" Joe went off again, and Archer let him go, knowing he would run down sooner or later. He looked at his watch. 7:50 Pacific; 8:50 Mountain. Early mornings and evenings had proved bumpy flying for the past few days, and Archer didn't expect that to change today. When Joe ran out of steam, he said, "OK, Joe. Again. Has anyone called the FBI?"

"No! Hell no! Didn't you hear what I just said?"

"I heard you, Joe. All right. That's up to the family. I just needed to know." He did some quick calculations in his head. "Yes. I'll take you to Colorado. Meet me at the strip at 11:15 Mountain. Confine yourself to one backpack."

"I'll be there." There was a pause. "Thank you, AJ." Joe hung up.

He sat on the edge of the bed thinking. Sara. She'd been in the dream. He knew her number by heart, though he had never dared dial it. He looked at the phone in his hand. "I didn't invite her into the dream," he reasoned. "She just showed up."

He dialed Tom Sevlakovs.

"Good morning," Tom answered.

"Not so," Archer said grimly, "Someone's taken Joe Skladany's granddaughter."

"Opal," Tom said. Through the phone, Archer felt Tom pull himself into "the mode," as he called it.

"What do you need from me, Captain?"

Archer opened his mouth to caution Tom that this wasn't a combat mission and shut it when he realized that he didn't know that to be true.

"Grab your ready pack, get to the strip and pull all extra weight out of the Mobius. There will be four adults and their packs aboard, pretty sure. I can't imagine Jess won't want to go. We're headed for western Colorado, the Uncompahgre Plateau. You and Jess jumped there a few years ago. We flew out of Delta — Blake Field, something like that — south of Grand Junction. You know it. High altitude, Ponderosa, juniper, sage and sandstone. Joe says the name of the campground they are staying at is Cottonwood, and the trail Opal was taken from begins there and runs down Mesa Creek Canyon. Pull the appropriate maps out of the collection."

"Gotcha."

"One more thing, Tom."

"What's that?"

"I've had a dream about this."

"Ahh. So, Captain, do the good guys win?"

"I don't know." He hesitated. "But Sara was in the dream."

"Sara." Tom at first was confused by the reference, but Archer waited.

"Oh," Tom finally said. He hadn't thought about Sara Cafferty a lot, but reckoned correctly that Archer must think about her quite often. "That Sara. Bear-fighter Sara."

"That's the one," Archer confirmed.

"So, Captain, how long's it been since you talked to her?"

"Fourteen months, give or take a week."

"Hmm. Interesting." He said the word in a way that made Archer flinch a bit. It was a private joke begun when they were in high school and a girl named Miranda was part of their circle. The way she said it always made Archer laugh, and they had adopted the word into their "secret code" of friendship. It had been a long time and some hard times since either of them had used the inflection Tom just had.

Some relationships erode over time and some stand the test. None had stood better than that between Archer MacClehan and Tomas Sevlakovs. For all the years they had known each other, since they were sophomores in high school, the responsibility of each to the other had been very clear. Archer's was to lead, confide and project; Tom's was to follow, advise and protect. The arrangement worked very well. In their senior year at Belt, Montana, High School, wearing the blue and gold of the Huskies, Tom was the back who protected Archer at quarterback on pass plays and ran for over half the rushing touchdowns made that year. The Huskies were 10 and 2 and runners up at State.

They had been in tandem for a long time. Through hard times, some downright nasty times, in fact, including the loss of their "interesting" girl, their friendship survived.

On this morning, Tom realized his verbal gaffe, but was gratified to hear Archer laugh.

"Yes," Archer said, "interesting, indeed."

Tom was relieved and happily surprised by his friend's response. "Shall I call Jesse?"

"I think I should."

"OK. See you at the strip." Tom hung up.

Archer dialed Jesse's number and got "Jesse Turnbull. Leave a message."

"Jess," he said, "something's come up. Tom and I are headed for Colorado in a few hours. You may wish to come with us. I'm at home. Call me as soon as you can."

He hung up and sat on the edge of the bed planning what he needed to take to Colorado. The dream came back to him, and he sifted through it. The coral snake. Very pretty. Very poisonous. It blinked on and off like a holograph. The word "virtual" came to mind. "Virtual," he said, out loud. "Hmm."

The vultures weren't virtual, though. But vultures are more opportunistic than predatory, and the one was quite happy with his backpack. The vultures weren't identical — one was more aggressive. He closed his eyes. Something was interesting about the arrow he released, the one that pulled the cord around the vulture's legs. He brought back that moment in the dream, recalled it as best he could. He saw in his mind's eye that the boy in the dream was holding a crossbow. He frowned. He had a crossbow, all right, but he'd never shot it. It was a curiosity he'd bought from an old man in a junk store a few years before on one of his trips to Nespelem. It was hanging on a wall in the living room. It didn't even have a bowstring.

Archer went and took it off the wall. It was home-made, he was sure, but elegantly and stoutly crafted and of such a size that it felt more like a Uzzi in his hand than a rifle. The bow was a pure curve only 18 inches long crafted from a piece of spring steel. The frame was maple. He couldn't see any way to cock it except by brute force, of which it might take about all he had by the look of it.

He considered what to use for a bowstring, and what might work as bolts for such a device. A thought came to him, and he took the crossbow to his shop and rummaged in a box under the bench. When he found what he was looking for, he could see that with a bit of modification, they would work perfectly. He found a hacksaw, a file and a can of fluorescent paint and began to work. Soon he had six dayglo green bolts.

Chapter Thirteen: A Last Bad Deed

"OK, kid. You can yell as much as you want now."

Adrian pulled the duct tape off of Opal's mouth as gently as he could, expecting a caterwaul to follow, but the girl in the back seat of the Tahoe just watched him intently, as if trying to see through his mask.

"You OK, kid?" he asked.

"When my grandpa catches you, he's going to skin you," she said.

Adrian laughed at her matter of fact manner. "Nobody's gonna to catch me, little girl, much less your old grandpa. You know why people get caught?"

"Why?" Opal asked.

" 'cause they don't know when to quit, kid. That's why." He pointed a finger at Opal. "You, kid, are my last bad deed. After you, I quit."

"You should have quit before, Mr. Bad Guy," she said, " 'cause my grandpa — and my dad — are going to skin you."

Adrian withdrew and shut the door, leaving Opal in the cage that the back of the Tahoe was. The back doors opened from the outside only, and an expanded metal grate locked into place just behind the front seats, another behind the back seat. The Tahoe hadn't been originally redesigned with full-on passenger restraint in mind, but necessity is the mother of invention. Adrian had found it increasingly necessary to transport people who didn't necessarily want to be transported and so had made the necessary modifications. No one had ever escaped.

Once she got over her initial terror — which had been profound — Opal had moved into a patient place. She was learning interesting things about herself. Being frightened was not debilitating as long as she didn't dwell on what she didn't know. She set about keeping track of things she did. She knew how to think, how to reason things out. She knew she only had limited facts to think about in this case of being kidnapped, which she was sure she was. She knew that kidnappers nearly always do it for money, and she knew that her parents both had lots of that. She knew also that her parents loved her enough to spend everything they had to get her back.

Two men were her kidnappers. They wore masks, but it was easy to tell them apart. One was tall and skinny and sort of — what was that word? feminate? something like that — he had a feminate way about him. *Skinny Man's a wuss*, she thought, *and a coward and a bully*. She liked the other man more, though she knew he was the more dangerous. Bad Guy was brave and not so mean, but he was also a bad, bad man. He was, Opal decided, the baddest of the two because he wasn't afraid to be as bad as he could be.

Bad Guy was the one who had grabbed her from behind. He must have had the duct tape laid out in his palm, she reasoned, because it was over her mouth as soon as she knew he was there. He was very strong, but also — what word did she want?

Careful. He was careful with her. He laid her head first over his right shoulder at her waist, reached around and grabbed her left wrist with his left hand and pulled her tight against his back, trapping her right arm between her body and his. She could hardly breathe, much less wriggle, but she was completely safe from falling. She could only see down, and she watched the backs of his legs and heels and the rock under his feet while her stomach and mind whirled in terror.

Bad Guy clamped Opal to himself and strode across a sheet of rock and into a small, shaded crack in the canyon wall. During this, her pack bumped against the back of her head and her bill cap fell off, which grieved her. Her grandpa had given her that hat, Forest Service green with Smokey the Bear on the front. Four strides into the crack, he stopped and put her down abruptly, settling her against the wall on her bottom with her legs out in front of her. His mask-covered face was very close to hers, and he said in a rough whisper, "Stay still! Do you understand?"

Opal nodded. He sat down opposite her with his knees up and his back against the other side of the tiny canyon. He pulled a big pistol out of a holster under his arm and laid it in his lap. He intently watched out the crack for a long time and finally pulled himself to his feet and put his pistol away. He reached down and helped Opal up.

"Don't run," he said quietly, and his pistol appeared so quickly in his hand that Opal blinked. "I don't want to have to shoot you. OK?"

Opal nodded, and he put the pistol away again. He pulled a length of nylon cord out of a pocket and said, "Tie this tight around your waist. Square knot."

Opal did as she was told, lapping the rope upon itself as her grandpa had shown her how many years before she couldn't remember. She could have tied a bos'n's for that matter or a half-hitch or slipknot.

Adrian examined the knot. "Good job, kid," he said and grabbed the leads to the knot and pulled, making the muscles of his forearms stand out, setting the knot hard. He tied a loop in the long lead and put the loop around his left wrist, leaving a length of eight feet between himself and Opal. Then, he led her out of the crack.

A few steps out of the crack, Bad Guy picked up her hat and put it back on her head. He had his own reasons — no clue left behind — but Opal was gratified. She secured the hat by pulling it down tight.

Opal soon learned to keep right behind him so the swing of his arm did not jerk her as they hiked. In defense of her sanity as much as for any other reason, Opal counted the seconds it took to get from where they had hidden to the camp above in the larger canyon. She didn't know why she would do that except it gave her something to think about instead of being scared. It took 2386 seconds from the time they stepped out of the crack in the sandstone until they reached the camp. The hike was not easy.

After coming out of where they had been hiding, they returned to the spot where the big rocks were, which took 173 seconds, and then continued on the trail she and Ross had been following. After 808 seconds, they began up a pile of broken red and yellow rock interspersed with sand and a few plants and shrubs growing out of it. It took 635 seconds to climb up that and into a crack much larger than the one they had hidden in before. 748 seconds later, Bad Guy said, "Coming in," and someone answered, "Come ahead." 22 seconds later, she met Skinny Man.

Skinny Man wore a mask, as did Bad Guy, but his was of desert camouflage material, grey and white, like the soldiers in Iraq wore. Bad Guy's mask was black. They found Skinny Man standing beside a camp table with a Coleman stove on it under a canopy made of the same sort of material his mask was made of. Behind him was some sort of big automobile draped with that same stuff. Off to one side stood a camouflaged wall tent.

"You brought her pack?" Skinny Man asked.

Bad Guy looked at Opal and laughed. "She brought it," he said.

"You should have left it!" He jerked it off Opal's back, wrenching her left arm. "What if it's got a Spot in it?"

"Mmmm!" Opal protested.

"Don't damage the goods," Adrian growled. "What do you mean, 'a spot' ?"

"Holy crap. Don't you know anything?" Skinny Man was highly disgusted, Opal could tell. "A GPS tracking beacon."

He began rummaging around in the pack and found Opal's phone. He flipped it open, turned it on and fiddled with it for a moment. "Tracking's off, thank God." He turned it off and dumped the rest of the pack's contents out and sorted through the water bottles, trail mix, protein bars and sunscreen. He pulled a small stuffed elephant out of the left water bottle holder and dropped it onto the ground at his feet. Opal lunged forward and snatched Alice out of the dirt, surprising everyone, including herself. She clamped the stuffed toy to her chest and glared at Skinny Man. If looks could kill, Adrian decided, Jack was a dead man. He decided he liked Opal. She was a good judge of character.

"Whoa," Skinny Man said, and took a step toward Opal, reaching for the elephant.

"Leave it alone," Bad Guy said, and Skinny Man gave the other man a withering look, but stayed his hand.

"It's a toy, for cryin' out loud," Bad Guy said. "Let her keep it."

Skinny Man relented with a grunt and continued digging through the pack. Satisfied that it didn't contain a tracking device, he stuffed the contents back in, willy-nilly, and tossed it against the canyon wall downstream of the Tahoe.

"All right, then. Let her keep it. Small comfort. Put her up so we can get out of these damned masks."

And that was when Bad Guy put her in the Tahoe under the camouflage, took the duct tape off her mouth and locked her in.

After he had withdrawn, Opal rubbed her sore shoulder and examined her little prison. The camouflage tarp covered the side and back windows, and a gray curtain hung on the other side of the grate in front. She wondered if she could pull it aside and sneak a look into the front seat, but decided she would wait a while. She didn't want to get caught peeking, and she didn't want to know what Skinny Man or Bad Guy looked like. She was easily able to extrapolate what exposure might mean to a kidnapper.

Across the grate behind the seat was a stack of tools, gear and luggage. She took mental inventory. An axe. A short-handled shovel. A hydraulic jack (the best kind, according to her grandpa.) Two tires on rims. Two red gas cans. Two blue water jugs. A box of food; canned goods, dried fruit, pasta. A backpack with an airline tag on it.

She squinted a bit. In the dim light she could make out a name on the tag: Jack Maxwell. This gave her a sudden chill. She realized that she now knew something she did not want to know.

Chapter Fourteen: Crossbow

The phone on the shop wall rang, and Archer, deep into his crossbow project, startled a bit and then picked it up.

"Colorado!" Jesse said, brightly. "But I haven't a thing to wear."

"Bring your tracking shoes, Jess," Archer said.

His grim tone brought Jesse immediately to attention, and she listened intently as he told her what he knew, which he had to admit, wasn't much. He didn't share the dream.

The most compelling reason Archer MacClehan had concerning a decision he had made long ago to not take Jesse Turnbull as that most intimate of partners was his unwillingness to share the Telling Dreams with her. That realization nearly made him cry, for it came at a moment when he was near changing his mind about Jesse, close to signaling her to come alongside, and that put the kibosh on that. In his bones, Archer knew it would be a betrayal of himself and of her, and if there was anything Archer knew for certain, it was to honor that knowledge, as tempting as it might be not to. He knew that whoever would share his bed and table would have to know about the dreams, and at the same moment, that Jesse was out of the loop until that time came.

After Archer had outlined the details, Jesse said simply, "When I'm ready, I'll swing by and get you, if you like."

It was an odd offer, because Archer's place was well out of the way of her route to the private strip where his plane resided, but it was an odd morning. Archer intuited that Jesse needed an assignment.

"That would be good," he said. "Make it about 10:15 Mountain. Stop and grab Tom at the strip. I'll have breakfast for you both."

After Jesse hung up, Archer lingered in the shop, trying to figure out an efficient way to cock the crossbow. He was still flummoxed by it when he went to make breakfast.

Chapter Fifteen: "Alpha Bi. . . ."

A*rcher's phone, which had already rung* a *great deal* that morning, this time rang four times before the answering machine picked up. A voice Sara feared she might have forgotten sailed across space to a point on the plateau where cell phones reliably worked. She realized she would know the rich baritone and its slight drawl even if it spoke to her from the sky, which it sort of was in that time and place.

"You've reached the MacClehan place, but I'm not in right now. Leave a message after the tone and I'll ..... beeeeeeeeep .... "

"Hang on a sec." It was a woman's voice, and Sara's heart threw itself against her sternum, nearly crushing the butterfly. There was a moment of low feedback as the person on the other end of the call turned the machine off.

"Hello?"

Sara fought off the urge to hang up. What had she expected? It was over a year since she'd spoken to Archer. Did she think he'd been in a deep freeze?

"Hello?" The woman sounded annoyed.

"Is, ah ... is Archer home?"

Sara thought — imagined? —she heard a caught breath.

"We're just leaving." The voice was flat and unwelcoming. Even as she waited for a bit of encouragement, for the woman to say, "Can I take a message?" Sara knew she would get none.

She screwed up her courage, as if it hadn't been already to nearly its fullest extent. Just getting the number from Information had gotten the butterfly wing-beats per minute into the low eighties. She misdialed three times before she got tickled and laughed hard enough to calm herself. The butterfly slowed to about 65.

She managed the fourth time to dial correctly, only to get this uninformative — the word "wench" came to mind.

She cleared her throat. "Um ... when do you expect he'll be home again?"

"I have no clue."

Sara was beginning to not care who this woman was or what she was to Archer.

"Would you take a message, please?"

"We're sort of in a hurry here. What's the message?"

"Tell him Sara Cafferty called."

There was silence, then, and finally Sara asked, "Did you get that?"

"Yes. I got it." The voice changed somehow — softened, Sara thought — and something in it was familiar. She suddenly felt like a great fool. She knew it was Jesse Turnbull, but it seemed Jesse did not want to be known, though Sara couldn't guess why.

But she could imagine and her imagination came out of the gate at a full gallop. Sara knew how Jesse felt about Archer, that she'd loved him forever. She'd also felt that she and Jesse were friends when they parted company at the end of the Great Grizzly Adventure, which is how Sara referenced the pack trip upon which she met Jesse, Tom and Archer. She had suspected that Jesse was even an ally, but 14 months is a long time; a long, long time. Still, there were things to do, ducks to get in order. And they still weren't, but she had waited as long as she could stand it — plus a couple of months — until "Today."

Maybe, as she had feared, she had waited too long.

"I'll tell him," the woman Sara knew was Jesse said, and Sara thought she could hear her heart breaking from 1,200 miles away.

"Jesse," she said. "Is that you?"

"Yes, it's me, Sara." Jesse's anger came searing across the phone line. "You pick a hell of a time to call."

"What — is everybody OK?"

"No. Not everybody is OK."

"What's wrong?"

In the background, a male voice — Tom's voice, Sara knew — called out, "Jesse, we gotta go!"

"Sara," Jesse continued, "I have to go." The phone grew still, and Sara fully expected that Jesse had hung up. She was ready to close her phone when she heard the sound of a deep breath being drawn in, like one might take before jumping into an icy mountain lake

"Try to remember this, dammit," Jesse said. "406-840-1324."

Click. Brrrrrrrrrrr.

Sara could only stare at her phone. That wasn't the number she'd just dialed. She flipped the phone shut to break the connection, and then back open, reciting the number out loud as she did, "840-1324, 840-1324." She was reasonably sure she had it right when she got it entered. She hit "Save," and when prompted, typed in "Lead Dog?"

She dialed the number.

"Jesse Turnbull. Leave me a message."

Sara hung up without waiting for the beep.

She flipped open the phone and scrolled through the contacts to "Lead Dog?" and backspaced through the name. With a grim little smile, she typed in "Alpha bi . . . " before she relented. Again, she backspaced through what she had entered and typed in "Jesse Turnbull."

Chapter Sixteen: Ready To Roll

A*t Rock Springs, Jesse watched Archer* fuel the Mobius from inside the terminal and checked phone messages. Sara had left two.

"Jesse, whatever you are up to — I mean, it sounds like you were in a big hurry this morning — this is important. I know this might be hard for you, but I need to speak to Archer, please. Would you have him call me at 928-321-6574. Please. Thanks."

And then.

"OK, friend. This is making me a little crazy. So bear with me. I have no idea what's going on, but after all these months of restraining myself, it was made very clear to me this morning that it was time to call Archer. You know how that can happen, Jess. So I call, and now I'm sitting here wondering what in the world is going on. It's like finally climbing out of the freezer and finding myself in the frying pan. Help! Somebody call me, please! 928-321-6574."

Outside the terminal window, Archer was moving the fuel nozzle to the port wing tank, so Jesse knew she had about 8 minutes. She dialed the number. The phone hardly rang once.

"Hello?"

"Hello, Sara."

"Jesse! Thank you, God! Is everyone all right. I mean, are you guys OK?"

"Yes, 'us guys' are OK, but one of our friends is not. I've got about six minutes before I have to get back in the airplane. Long story short is that his granddaughter was taken this morning and we are on our way to Colorado to see what we can do to help."

There was silence.

"Sara? Did I lose you?"

"Taken. What do you mean 'taken?' "

"Someone kidnapped her somewhere in Colorado early this morning, and we are headed there now."

"Where in Colorado?" Sara asked the question very carefully.

"We're flying into Delta. And then headed into the Umcompagre, it sounds like."

"Delta. Who's going to pick up you there?"

"The little girl's mom and her boyfriend will meet us there. Hopefully, we can rent some kind of rig, too, as there are four of us."

"You, Tom, Archer and . . . ?"

"The little girl's grandpa, Joe Skladany."

"Would a crew cab four-wheel drive pickup come in handy?"

"Perfect. But how can you arrange that?"

"Jesse. I don't know why or how, but I'm staying in Montrose right now."

"Montrose."

"It's about 50 miles from Delta."

"What!?"

"I know. I *know.* I don't quite understand this, but . . ."

"Sara, I'm sorry, but I gotta go. We should be in Delta by 6:30 latest. And you will meet us there?"

Sara's butterfly stretched and then fluttered its wings. She pulled in a deep breath.

"Sara. I've gotta go. What are you gonna do?"

Sara let the breath out, and with it came "I'll be there."

"See you then."

"That will be interesting," Sara said, but she was talking to herself. Jesse had closed her phone and was running for the airplane.

She looked at her watch. 3:00. In three hours, plus 30 minutes, she would walk back into a world she feared she might never enter again, the place where Archer MacClehan was the lead dog and to be part of his circle of friends, one best be ready to roll. That was how Jesse had explained it in what seemed like one rather long lifetime ago, although it was a paltry 14 months.

"Holy Samoley!" Sara nearly yelled it. Rather than risk missing a return call, she had been sitting in a cell pocket she knew to be dependable since leaving the original message; nearly three hours. She was almost two hours from Montrose, and it was another hour from there to Delta. She had no idea where the airport was. She ran for the truck. She briefly wondered if she would have time for a shower. "To heck with that, Sara," she told herself. "You said you'd be there, and you will be — aaack — dusty jeans, armpit circles, hat hair and all." She jammed the Tundra into low and began grinding up canyon toward the top of the plateau.

The Mobius climbed out of Rock Springs and swung to a line a bit east of south. Jesse was in the right seat. Joe and Tom were in the back with Tom behind Jesse to keep the weight even in the plane. To make conversation easier, everyone had a headset on, and Jesse wondered if she should ask the men in the back seat to take theirs off. She wasn't quite sure how to approach this subject. It was a bit on the delicate side, and it was a hell of a time to be broaching it. Finally, she just waded in.

"AJ, I know you have a lot on your mind already, but I need to tell you something."

"What did we leave behind?"

Jesse and Tom both laughed. She was famous for not remembering every little thing.

"No, AJ. We left nothing behind, but there is a complicating factor waiting in Delta — or will be when we get there."

"What's that?"

Jesse took a deep breath.

"More like who's that. Sara."

Archer flinched, but he didn't look surprised. He looked over his shoulder at Tom, as if checking to see if he knew who this Sara was.

"You know. Sara Cafferty?"

"Yep, Jess. I know. Sara." He let out a low whistle. "Holy Samoley."

"She called this morning just as we were leaving, and since we've played a bit of phone tag. I caught up with her while we were on the ground in Rock Springs. Do you have any idea what she's doing in Colorado."

"I haven't talked to Sara since last summer."

"Well. We never talked about it. I just thought maybe . . . Oh, hell. I don't know."

"OK. We'll find out more when we get there."

"Who's Sara Cafferty?" Joe asked from the back seat.

And what is she doing in Colorado? thought the three others in the plane, independently and simultaneously.

Nobody felt up to trying to explain it all to Joe, but Tom finally volunteered, "A friend of ours we met last summer."

To everyone in the plane except Joe, that was a totally inadequate explanation.

Chapter Seventeen: Bathroom Break

"H*ey! I have to go to the bathroom!"*

"Oh, Christ!" Jack was not ready to deal with being a custodian, even if the "guest" *was* worth two mil.

"Hey. I have to go really bad!"

Adrian was pulling on his mask. *Some things, you don't think about ahead of time,* he thought.

"Get your mask on," he told Jack. "Hang on, kid, I'll be right there."

He stepped under the cover and opened the door. "Number one or number two?" he asked.

"Both!"

"Fine." He closed the door.

"Hey!"

"Let me get a shovel, kid. Jesus . . ."

He stepped to the back of the Tahoe and returned a moment later with a short-handled shovel and a roll of toilet paper.

"OK, kid. C'mon." He grabbed the rope that was still knotted around her waist. "Follow me."

"You can't watch," she said.

"We'll find you a big bush," he said.

They walked up the canyon a short ways and found a juniper of sufficient size to give Opal some privacy. Adrian dug a cat hole, left her with the shovel and roll of paper, and then carefully studied the wall of the canyon for a few minutes.

"Are you done yet?" he finally asked.

"Not yet!" Opal was testy.

Adrian sighed. *This is like having a dog,* he thought, *only a little worse.*

"Done," she finally said.

"Cover it up," he told her, and listened to the shovel scrape.

"OK."

He reeled her in and took the shovel and paper back and led her back to the Tahoe.

"I'm hungry," she said as he put her back in the cage. "And, I need a drink."

Adrian closed the door and went away. A few minutes later, he came back with a Nalgene bottle out of her pack, her bag of trail mix and an apple. When he gave them to her, he noted that Alice was buckled into the far seat.

"You OK, kid?" he asked.

"Just fine," she answered, "for being kidnapped."

He laughed, and closed the door.

Opal sat quietly for a while, listening. She heard the men say something to each other, and Skinny Man laughed. Bad Guy said something that she couldn't make out, but she knew he was somewhat angry. Then it got quiet.

Finally, she allowed herself to retrieve the treasure she had found beneath the juniper bush. She tugged up her left pant leg, and pulled the point of the rusted spike out of her boot top. She had managed to work the big nail (*Twenty-penny?* she wondered.) out of the rotted piece of wood it was imbedded in.

Someone had built something here long ago, and now it was rotted into the ground, but she had found a part of it. "Just a piece of an old something-or-other," Grandpa Joe would have said, as he did when he found artifacts like this one in the woods in Montana.

Just a piece of an old something-or-other that might get her out of the Tahoe, should push come to shove. That's what Opal was thinking as she stuffed the spike out of sight between the seats. Her heart slowed down then, and she took a big drink of water and began picking the peanuts out of the trail mix. Next would be the raisins. Then the cashews. Then the M&Ms would be all that were left.

Save the best for last, she thought.

She stuck her fingers between the seats and felt the big nail resting there. *Next,* she thought, considering the far window, *I'll need something to hit it with.*

Chapter Eighteen: Delta Arrival

T*hey were early getting into Delta* — the Mobius touched down at 6:17 Mountain. The sun dropped close to the bulk of the plateau to the west, and the ranges to the east were highlighted in spectacular fashion. Waiting in the late day sun at the edge of the runway were Ross's Explorer, a nine-passenger Dodge van and a dark green crew-cab four-by-four Toyota pickup. Between the van and the Explorer were seven people, most of whom looked lost to Tom. Leaning against the pickup was a slender woman with red hair. Jesse, Tom and Archer recognized her immediately.

Of all those waiting, only Sara looked to Tom like she was where she was supposed to be.

Archer swung the Mobius in next to a Citation jet and ran through the shutdown procedure, switching off the

Number 2 engine last and then the radio. The sudden quiet was as welcome as it was foreign. It always struck Archer as a reminder of the silence of the backcountry. As much as he loved to fly, he was grateful for it every time.

Jesse was first on the ground. She had the cargo hatch open and was pulling out packs as the other three disembarked. The crew of the Citation — who might have thought their passengers were in Colorado for a funeral — were herded into the van by its driver and taken off to a motel in Delta. Left behind were the rest of those Tom thought lost: Helen, Ross, Kelly and Sabrina.

The next few minutes were a mélange of greetings and introductions. Sara hung back, but Tom went to greet her. Next, Jesse detached herself and went to say hello, and finally Archer. His heart did small leaps as he walked across the tarmac, and he willed it to settle down as Sara and Jesse exchanged a tentative embrace. They broke as he approached and turned to meet him.

As solemn as the occasion was, Archer couldn't keep his crooked grin in check. "Ms. Cafferty. A pleasure." He held out his hand.

Sara was equally formal as she took it. "Mr. MacClehan. Likewise."

In the interest of not tipping her hand, Sara tried her best not to radiate the unexpected joy she felt to see this big galoot, but her butterfly was fully awakened by the spark that jumped the space between their hands long before they met in a firm shake. And she realized that it wasn't just the lead galoot she was happy to see, but the other two galoots as well. Being reserved wasn't working well for any of them. They were all grinning.

There is something about surviving an event like the Great Grizzly Adventure that forms a bond among the survivors. And these four were the survivors. None would ever forget the others, no matter how far apart they might be, and reunion would always be about the mutual joy of being alive and the recognition that without each of the others, that might not be the case.

"What are you doing in Colorado?" Archer asked.

"Geology research. Working on a thesis."

"Did you get whiplash from that change of direction?"

Sara laughed. "Getting thrown from a bear will do that to a girl."

"AJ. I think they're waiting for us." It was Jesse who interceded.

Archer looked over his shoulder. The van was pulling away and Joe and the rest of them were looking in their direction with some expectation.

"Let's see what's up," he said, even though it hurt to move back into the reality of the situation. He walked toward the other group, and as he did, he got the distinct feeling that a team, *his* team, was following him. He'd never felt quite that way before, and it scared him a little bit. *Slow down, MacClehan,* he thought. *You have a lot to do, I think.*

Archer and his crew met Helen, Ross, Kelly and Sabrina. Archer, Kelly and Helen knew each other through Joe. The rest of them were strangers to each other.

To Tom, all of them appeared shaky. Helen was gray and exhausted, nearly in shock. She would need a sleeping pill tonight to make it through tomorrow. He made a mental note to see that she got one. Joe was still on the edge of rage. Kelly looked lost and Sabrina seemed to be holding him up. It was Ross that worried him most, though. Ross was vacant. He was gone, and something would have to be done to bring him back.

Tom also saw accurately that there was no leader in the others. They were all waiting for someone else to tell them what to do. He looked at Archer.

"Captain?"

Archer understood the inflection in Tom's voice and the expectation that went with it. "All right, Sergeant," he answered.

If anyone else noticed the reference to rank, Sara hadn't a clue of who it might have been, but she was somewhat surprised by the resignation in Archer's voice.

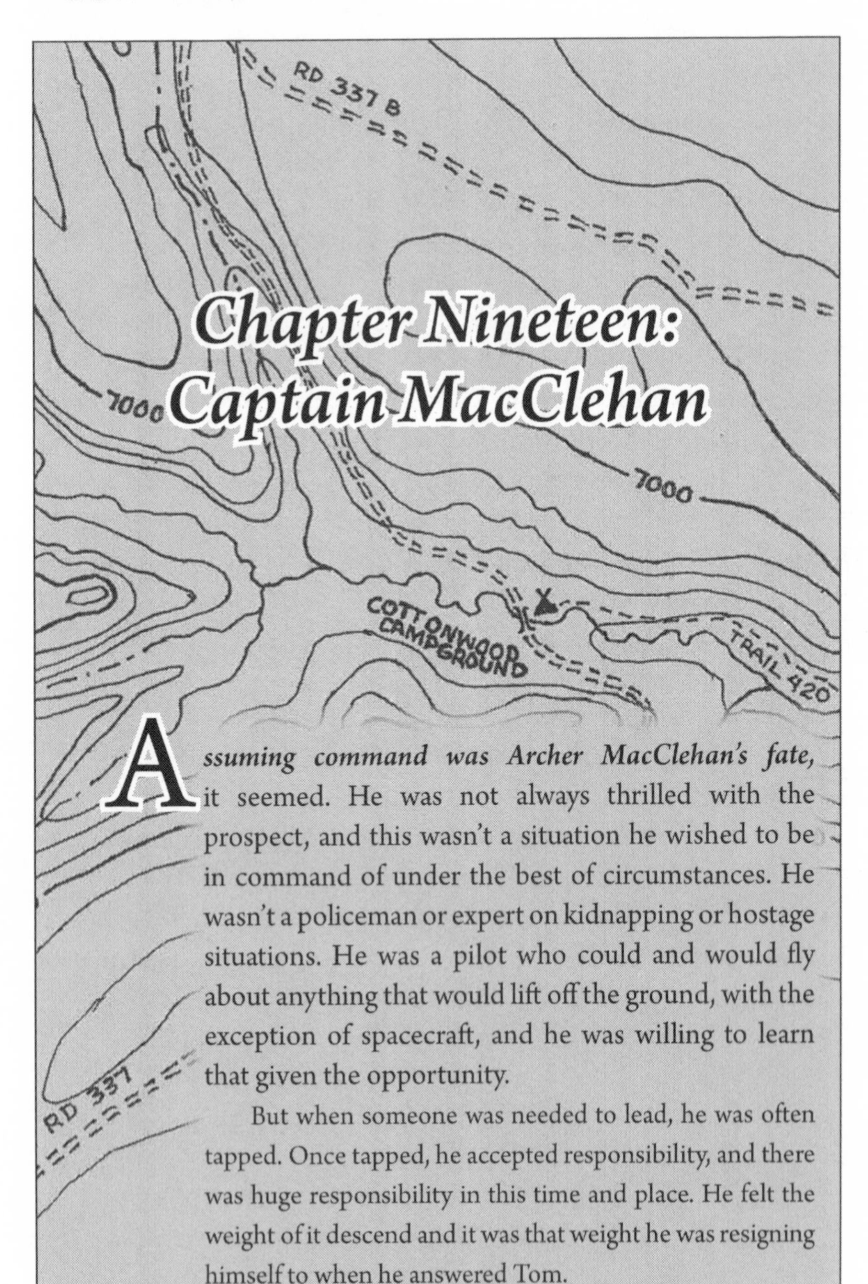

Chapter Nineteen: Captain MacClehan

Assuming command was Archer MacClehan's fate, it seemed. He was not always thrilled with the prospect, and this wasn't a situation he wished to be in command of under the best of circumstances. He wasn't a policeman or expert on kidnapping or hostage situations. He was a pilot who could and would fly about anything that would lift off the ground, with the exception of spacecraft, and he was willing to learn that given the opportunity.

But when someone was needed to lead, he was often tapped. Once tapped, he accepted responsibility, and there was huge responsibility in this time and place. He felt the weight of it descend and it was that weight he was resigning himself to when he answered Tom.

"Someone needs to fill me in on details," he said.

A few minutes later, under the glare of florescent lights in the airport terminal's small lobby, Helen mutely laid the baggie Ross had found in the trail on a table in front of Archer. He read the first page through the clear plastic as Tom, Kelly and Joe looked over his shoulder.

"Christ almighty," Joe said, and turned away.

Archer said to Tom, "Tom, take Joe for a walk."

As Tom turned after the older man stalking away, Ross caught his attention. "Ross. Why don't you come along, too? Walk might do you good."

Ross looked surprised, but nodded and fell in behind Tom. Archer watched them follow Joe outside before turning back to the group.

"Who's handled this?" Archer asked. He was reading the back page of the note.

"We've been very careful with it," Helen answered, as if from outer space. "Nobody's opened the bag."

"Do you have the money?"

"In that case." Kelly pointed to a medium-sized roll-around suitcase.

Archer nodded. "Their intentions are clear enough. There seems to be no way to communicate with them. I don't see anything to do but meet their requests."

"And then what?" Kelly asked.

"I don't know yet." Archer looked off to the west. "They're out there. I've flown over it, but that's not like being in it. What's the terrain like?"

"Eroded sandstone upthrust," Sara volunteered from behind Kelly, "riven with canyons that run primarily east or west off the crest, which is about 9,000 feet. Many but not all of these have either a road or a significant trail running through them. The canyons are fed by smaller arroyos, many of which are plenty big enough to hide a camp in. By the nature of the rock, the canyons and arroyos are steep-sided with vertical and even overhung walls in many places. Water is scarce, particularly this time of year, although there is still quite a bit in Mesa Creek. The ridges between the canyons are relatively open — sage, piñon and juniper on gentler grades — with some big grazing allotments, but still broken with varying levels caused by migration of streams over the centuries. Lots of little hidey-holes, and four-wheel drive tracks everywhere. BLM and the Forest

Service have some officially designated roads. The crest road, which runs the length of the plateau, is a good-quality Forest Service haul road — they've logged a lot of ponderosa from up on top over the years. Unless you are familiar with the place, though, it's a great place to get good and lost, GPS and all."

"Nice report, Ms. Cafferty," Archer said. Even in the current situation, he could not help but admire how the slim young woman across the room handled herself.

"Thank you, Mr. MacClehan," she answered, pleased that he was pleased.

"Just who are you?" Sabrina asked from beside Kelly "And why are you here?"

Sara weighed her answer. "Sara Cafferty. I've been doing geology work here for the past three weeks. In Mesa Creek, as a matter of fact, but way above the campground. I'm, . . ." She paused briefly, looking at Archer, then Jesse. "I'm a friend of Jesse, Tom and Archer . . . AJ. They needed transportation and I volunteered my truck."

Nobody questioned that and Sara was glad. She didn't want to have to explain the string of coincidences that had led her to this place in time.

"The campground," Kelly said.

"We're camped at Cottonwood Campground." Helen said.

"That's where we should be headed right soon if we're going to deliver the money tomorrow," said Archer.

This caused a small stir in the group.

"Yes. You're right," Helen said. She turned and looked to the west. "It takes a couple of hours to get there. It's where the trail begins."

"The trail where the girl was taken?" Sara asked.

"Her name is Opal," Archer interjected and Helen winced.

"Yes," Helen answered. "Yes, that's right. Her name is Opal."

"How far from the campground did it happen, Helen?" Archer asked.

"I don't know," she said, and it spoke to her complete state. Helen knew nothing about much of anything at the moment. Her world had exploded 12 hours before and the pieces were still flying away from each other. She began to cry.

"You'll have to ask Ross," she said and looked around. "Where is Ross?"

Ross was with Tom Sevlakovs and Joe Skladany, trailing them along the edge of the tarmac as they walked slowly down the runway. Joe was again enraged, railing against the kidnappers and Helen and Ross. Ross was still as numb as he had been since morning.

Tom paused in a pool of light under a mercury vapor light and said, "Joe. You better get a hold on that. You need to be thinking more clearly if you're going to be helpful."

Joe took this moment to turn and confront Ross. "What the hell kind of man are you, anyway, to let them take that little girl without so much as a wimper?"

Ross wasn't on the same planet nor in the same time frame. He was still stuck in the moment when he'd first picked the ziplock bag off the trail, reading the first sentence of the ransom note. He was trying to wake up from that moment — willing it to be a wee bit of a nightmare — and find Opal standing in the trail. Ross was living then and there and trying to mold a new reality, and so had trouble understanding Joe.

His silence caused Joe to grab the front of his shirt. He pulled Ross up close and yelled into his face, "Answer me!"

Tom stepped in and pushed the older man away. "Don't do that Joe. He's not to blame for this."

"Like hell he isn't. He's the one who brought her down here." He turned back to Ross. "Kelly never would have let her be taken. He would have died first."

Ross was waking up, now. Tom could see it. It was like watching an old radial airplane engine start, first one cylinder, then another, then a rough chorus of noise until all cylinders fell into rhythm and things smoothed out. He spoke his first words since Tom had arrived in Delta.

"Mr. Skladany. If I had opportunity to stop Opal being taken, I would have done my damnedest — but I didn't. One minute she was there. The next she was gone. Yes. I'm responsible, and I'll have to live with it no matter how this turns out. I'm sorry."

"You're sorry, alright," Joe said. His volume increased. "You been trying to supplant Opal's dad ever since you met her. Meddling between a child and her father. You should know Opal hates your guts for that. Why in hell would she want to go hiking with you, anyway? You and her mom must have forced her."

"Helen doesn't force Opal to do anything, Mr. Skladany, except go to her room when she's disrespectful."

Ross's voice came out cold and hard, and Tom could almost see the hackles rise on him. *This is good,* Tom thought, *but it can't go too far.*

"I stay out of the role of parent," Ross continued, "or try to. And, Opal doesn't hate my guts, Mr. Skladany. She despises them. But I don't care too much, because I think she's a grand little girl who will grow up one day and get over the hurt of her dad leaving her mom. When that happens, maybe we will get to be friends."

"What do you mean, 'her dad leaving her mom'?" Joe was shouting. "Helen's the one who filed for divorce. Kelly never saw it comin'."

Ross looked evenly at Joe. "Maybe you should get your son in a corner sometime and ask him what really happened between him and Helen. You might be surprised."

Oops. Tom thought. *Too far.*

Joe lunged for Ross, swinging a roundhouse right, but Ross was now awake. He stepped inside the blow, turned his back and levered Joe over himself by Joe's outstretched arm. Joe landed on his back on the runway and the air went out of him. He lay still for a long moment, trying to get his breath back. Ross stood over him, waiting for Joe to inhale. When he finally did, Ross stepped back.

"I'm going to see what needs to be done," he said to Tom. He turned and began back toward the terminal building.

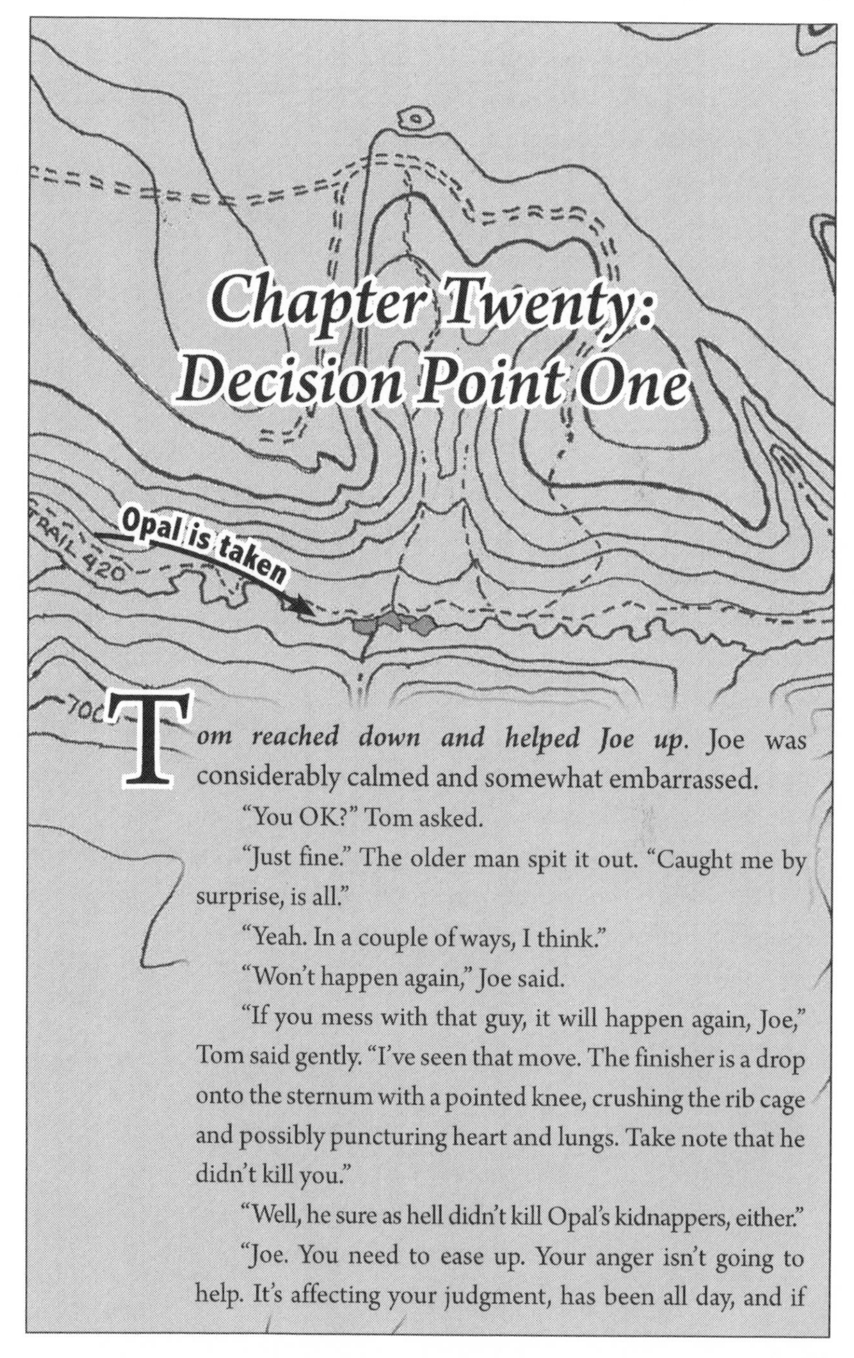

Chapter Twenty: Decision Point One

T*om reached down and helped Joe up*. Joe was considerably calmed and somewhat embarrassed.

"You OK?" Tom asked.

"Just fine." The older man spit it out. "Caught me by surprise, is all."

"Yeah. In a couple of ways, I think."

"Won't happen again," Joe said.

"If you mess with that guy, it will happen again, Joe," Tom said gently. "I've seen that move. The finisher is a drop onto the sternum with a pointed knee, crushing the rib cage and possibly puncturing heart and lungs. Take note that he didn't kill you."

"Well, he sure as hell didn't kill Opal's kidnappers, either."

"Joe. You need to ease up. Your anger isn't going to help. It's affecting your judgment, has been all day, and if you don't get a handle on it, it will get in everybody's way." Tom looked after Ross. "You don't have to believe me, but from what I just saw, if that man had opportunity to stop it, Opal would not have been taken, at least not while he was able to fight."

Joe said nothing. The drop onto the runway had hurt more than his pride. He was going to have trouble breathing for a few days, he knew already. And what the hell did that mean, "get your son in a corner?" He began slowly back up the runway, and Tom paced him.

Back at the terminal, Ross walked back into the group as Helen asked her question.

"Right here." He went to her side. "Sorry. I was gone for a bit."

And now, you're back, Archer thought. He didn't know what had happened on the walk with Tom and Joe, but it was easy to see something had. This was not the vacant shell that Tom had pulled along on his way out the door.

"Ross," Archer said, "Sorry, but I need to ask you. How far from the campground was Opal taken?"

"Who are you?"

"AJ MacClehan. I'm a friend of Opal's Grandpa Joe. How far, Ross? The note says at exactly 4 p.m. tomorrow, we need to have the money at the spot Opal was taken. What time do we need to leave camp to achieve that?"

In his mind, Ross went back to the last time he looked at his watch on the hike. He is standing on the downstream side of the boulder field, waiting for Opal and impatient to go faster. The line of sun is approaching from the top edge of the plateau, but hasn't gotten to them quite yet. Upstream, the line of light is still a half-mile away. He yells for Opal to hurry up. He looks at his watch. It's 7:10.

"Opal was taken at ten after seven," he said, " so. . . "

Sara was doing math in her head. "You yelled her name."

Ross stared at her, and so did everyone else.

"How do you know that?" Sabrina asked.

"I heard you. I was working in the upper canyon. The sound carried up the creek."

"Yes. I yelled her name," Ross said, focusing on Sara. "Who are you?"

Sara explained once again her presence, trying to keep it as simple as possible. *If I tell the truth, the whole truth and nothing but the truth, someone is going to think I'm nuts,* she thought. *I mean someone besides me, because this is definitely nuts.*

Archer walked to a window and looked off to the west. The sun was set now, and the top of the plateau marked the passage of day into night, a line where black met heliotrope. His thoughts went to the little girl out there somewhere in that dark bulk, and he said a silent prayer for her. The weight of it all settled more deeply on him. He turned back to the group as Tom and Joe walked in. He was surprised by how old Joe had suddenly become, and that brought a question to his mind.

"There's something we need to decide right now," Archer said to the group. "Others can advise, but only three people get a vote; Kelly, Helen and Joe. Majority rules."

"What's that?" Joe asked.

"Shall we call the FBI?"

He expected an explosive "No!" from Joe but didn't get it. He looked at his friend, who seemed deep in thought. Something had changed.

Kelly and Helen both stared at the note on the table. Helen chewed on her lower lip and looked at Ross. Ross was looking at Joe.

"Joe?" Ross said.

Joe looked at Ross in surprise and then at the others. Tears came to his eyes. "I'm sorry, but I don't know what to do."

"Kelly?" Archer asked.

"They said they'll kill her."

"Is that a 'yes' or a 'no?' " Archer asked. Kelly looked at his feet, then back at Archer.

"What do you think?" Kelly asked.

"I can't decide for you, Kelly."

"But what do you *think*?" pressed Helen.

Archer looked at Tom, who was looking right at him. When they made eye contact, Tom drooped his eyes closed and dropped his chin to his chest as if he were asleep. He nearly immediately picked his head up again, but Archer knew exactly what he meant. He searched his memory of the dream and there were no police; just he and Sara; the vultures, the coral snake and Opal; and the native man's admonitions and promises.

"I think," Archer said slowly, looking from Sara to Jesse to Tom, all standing together by now, "that we will have to do this ourselves."

Something stirred in the group then, like a breeze through an aspen grove bringing the leaves to action. Each person there, even Helen in her numbness, felt it like a light charge of electricity running across their skin. They all woke a bit from the nightmare, and each, for whatever reason, felt some bit of hope. It was now in their own hands, and each took what part of it they could. To one extent or another, they all stood ready.

Chapter Twenty-One: The Money

"H*ow far to the drop point,* Ross?" Archer asked again.

"At a normal hiking pace, an hour," Ross said. He was definite, and both Archer and Tom were glad that he was.

"So, the money needs to leave the campground by 3:00 latest," Archer said.

"Who will deliver it?" Kelly asked.

"It will have to be me," said Ross. "I'm the one who knows where the spot is."

Archer looked again out at the edge of light along the top of the plateau. "I'll likely be going with you."

Sara didn't like the idea of Archer going with the money, but she bit her tongue. It was neither the time nor her place to question Archer on that, but she was cognizant of the strength of her feelings. For the first time since the Mobius had landed, she allowed herself to really take a good look at the lead dog.

He wasn't as tall as she remembered him, a bit under six feet, maybe; but still lean and possessed of sky-blue eyes and jet-black hair. Yes, this really was the guy who had saved her from the bear; the same guy she had saved from the same bear. They had saved each other, and she'd never quite thought of it that way. The hair on her arms rose of its own accord as a chill swept through her. He was talking, giving orders, which he was so damnably good at, but all she heard was the timbre of his voice. Her heart rate hit 80 before she noticed the acceleration. She forced herself to throttle back. *Down, girl. Sit. Stay,* she told herself. She took a deep breath, and made herself translate the sound into words, which was good, because it appeared that he was talking to her.

"Is that a personal pickup or a company pickup, Sara?"

"Personal."

"Do you mind if we requisition it?"

"That's why I'm here," she said. *Among other myriad reasons,* she thought to herself.

"Where are you staying?"

"By all appearances," she answered, "at Cottonwood Campground tonight."

That settled, Sara, Tom and Jesse went to load gear into the pickup. Tom was pleased to see Sara had thought to bring her camping gear as well as what appeared to be an extra sleeping bag. He was certain that Kelly and Sabrina were without, and they returned to the terminal to see what needed to be done about that.

When they walked in, Kelly was hefting a suitcase onto a table in the waiting room. He opened the case to reveal stack upon stack of bills wrapped in white sleeves, stacks of 250, ten packets of 25 bills each.

With authority, Tom reached in and pulled a stack of 100-dollar bills out. He riffled them with his thumb and watched the corners fly by, a flip-book that told the story that these were randomly packed, used bills, practically untraceable by serial number.

He tucked the packet back in and levered out a similar stack of 50s and read its story.

"What do you think?" Archer asked.

"Interesting," Tom said. He put the 50s back and said to Kelly, "You must have friends in the banking business."

"Yes, thank God!" Helen answered with more enthusiasm than she had displayed during the whole rest of the evening.

Tom gave her an odd look that Archer caught and Helen did not. Sara saw it too, and intuited that Tom was thinking about how difficult it might be to put together $2,000,000 in 100s, 50s and 20s on short notice without using new bills.

"Have you counted it?" Tom pulled a packet of 20s out.

"Twice. " It was Sabrina. "$1,500,000 in 100s, $450,000 in 50s, $50,000 in 20s."

Sara's math brain came online. A few moments later, out popped the answer: "Fifty-nine pounds, plus or minus."

"How do you know that?" It was Kelly who asked, but it was apparent that everyone wanted to know the answer. In fact, all were nearly gaping at Sara, who wished she had kept her mouth shut. She decided, though, to go ahead and show her work.

"Our currency weighs almost exactly a gram per bill," she explained. "Four-hundred-fifty-three grams to a pound. Twenty-six-thousand-five-hundred bills. Four-fifty — just to make it easier — into 26,500 is a bit under 59."

Sara glanced at Jesse, who had a cat-who-ate-the-canary expression. She was stifling a laugh and when their eyes met, Jesse grinned. "Nice computing, Ms. Math Whiz."

Sara grinned back at Jesse and said in a Dr. Frankenstein tone. "De numbers, dey stick in my head. I have to get dem out."

"This doesn't seem to be a time for jokes," Sabrina said, but Jesse snorted and Archer grinned and shook his head.

Kelly began to close the case, but Archer stopped him. "They want the money in a backpack. Mine's stout enough, so let me grab it. Also, I want a look at the map before we drive in."

While Archer emptied his pack into a box in the back of the Tundra, Tom retrieved the roll of maps from the Mobius and found the appropriate USGS quad map. Tom spread the map on the table that held the money.

"Here's the campground," Archer said, pointing to Cottonwood. "Where on this map do we leave the money, Ross?"

Ross looked for a moment, tracing the trail downstream with a finger. "We were just above these pools," he said, "so it must be about here."

The Montana crew plus Sara were all map people, and it was apparent to each of them the few places where the kidnappers might be hiding, unless the bad guys had hiked in from the Gunnison, which was unlikely by sheer distance. There were three spots within reasonable walking distance of the spot where Opal was taken where the canyon offered access to the higher country around it. Two of those were larger coulees, one on each side of the main canyon, and the third was a steep trail that left the Mesa Creek trail a mile below the oasis. The mouth of the southern tributary was a half-mile upstream of the spot. The side canyon on the north was just downstream of the pools.

Tom brought out a Colorado atlas, which was larger scale, and they pored over the country around the canyon for roads and trails. There was a BLM road on the highlands at both sides of the canyon. The one on the north was the closer to the rim. Both side canyons had a road near their upper ends and appeared large enough to drive a vehicle into. The trail topped the canyon wall where the BLM road on the north ended.

"My guess is they're here," Sara said, and she pointed to the side canyon on the north.

"How so?" Kelly asked.

"For one thing, the trail runs along the side of the canyon this arroyo opens into. For another, this one is downstream of where Opal was taken and in the opposite direction of where the money will be coming from. It's also plenty big to hide a camp in, while the trailhead at the top of the canyon is very exposed."

"The canyon on the south wall — why not there?" Archer asked.

Ross spoke up. "The main canyon bottom would be hard to cross laterally in that area. It's thick with juniper, tamarisk and Russian olive. It's not user friendly, for sure."

"All right," Archer said. "Before we go looking — or anywhere — it would be good for someone to make a run to the store. We've quite a crew to feed."

"I know where the store is at least," said Sara. "Who wants to go with?"

Jesse popped up her hand. "What else do we need? Kelly? Sabrina?"

Sabrina looked up from her phone and closed it. "Sorry," she said. "Trying to keep up with work a bit. We need sleeping bags and a tent, but where do we get those at this time of night?"

"You might be surprised what they sell at a Delta grocery store," Jesse said.

"You've been here before?" Sara was surprised.

"Have parachute, will travel," Jesse answered.

"Oh, yes," Sara said as they headed for the door, "how is the smoke jumping business?"

"Falling," Jesse said, and they both laughed. A grumpy-looking Sabrina followed them out.

"What do you mean, 'go looking'," Ross asked. "Would it do us any good to know where they are? What could we do about it? And how would we find out, anyway?"

"Always good to know where the bad guys are in any situation," Archer said "but can we find out without jeopardizing Opal? What do you think, Tom?"

Tom was looking intently at the quad map.

"It will take a few hours."

"What are you thinking?"

"They let us out here," his finger hit the map "and we go for a walk."

Chapter Twenty-Two: The Banker

The banker who Helen — and Kelly — was grateful to know was Jillian Dumas. The ties between the three of them were perhaps the only ones that survived the divorce pretty much intact, reason being that neither Helen nor Kelly knew the depth of the other's relationship with "the prettiest banker in Seattle," as Kelly called her.

Jillian was an investment banker and a financial adviser to Helen and Kelly when they were married. She made sure she remained both neutral and supportive when the Big D came along, staying out of the personal stuff and still being a personable, helpful and resourceful friend. Jillian did not like losing clients of any kind for any reason, particularly clients who suddenly had more money than they knew what to do with.

Kelly's assessment of her may have been superficial, but he was not wrong. Jillian was indeed beautiful. She bore a striking resemblance to a young Elizabeth Taylor, right down to the violet eyes — strategically augmented with contact lenses. She cultivated her beauty to her advantage as a banker because first and foremost that's what she was. God help the man who sat across from her at a negotiating table and forgot that.

After the call from Joe — Helen trusted her ex-father-in-law much more than her ex-husband and had left it up to Joe to tell Kelly — Kelly's mind was whirling and trying to land on what to do. Just after 8:00 a.m. in Capolis Beach, Jillian called him.

"Helen called," she said, "and told me what's up. If there's some way I can help . . . "

"Oh, Jesus, yes you can help! Where can we get that much cash?"

Joe had asked nearly the same question after Helen revealed the demands. "Where in hell are we going to get that kind of cash?"

Helen's first thought was of Jillian, with the sure knowledge that Jillian would know just where to find it. Jillian also knew that it was essential that the money be apparently untraceable. All she had to do was move a million dollars out of each of Kelly's and Helen's cash accounts — accomplished electronically after some last-minute details were taken care of— and turn digital records into a pile of printed pieces of linen, six-and-an-eighth by two-and-five-eighths inches each.

She wasted no time. An hour after hanging up and five minutes after the bank opened, she quietly removed $2 million from a pile of cash in her downtown bank's main vault.

"Someone's buying a sailboat," Jillian told the teller as she handed him the authorization she herself had worked up. "The seller wants cash."

It felt odd to walk down Beacon Avenue dragging 60 pounds of money in a roll-around suitcase, but at 9:15 Pacific time, she hefted the case into the back of her Audi and headed for the private terminal at Boeing Field.

Three hours and six phone calls with Jillian, Helen and Joe later, Kelly and Sabrina drove into Bowerman Airport at Hoquiam and found waiting the

Citation Jillian had promised. While the co-pilot lifted their luggage aboard, Kelly and Sabrina strapped down in the private cabin behind the flight deck. Five minutes later, they were rolling down the tarmac and 30 minutes after that, Portland slid under their starboard wing and the remains of Mount Saint Helens appeared to port. Neither noticed. They were busy counting the money in the suitcase Jillian had secured in the cabin when she dispatched the jet from Boeing Field to Hoquiam.

Chapter Twenty-Three: A Windmill

It was well dark by now, and in the canyon where the Tahoe was parked, the tent reverberated with Jack's snoring. Adrian contemplated taking his bag and finding a quieter spot. Stopping him was the thought of a snake joining him, a thought he did not like. He contemplated more drastic measures, but they didn't have the money yet, and Jack was necessary until they did.

He considered sleeping in the front seat of the Tahoe, but he didn't like the idea of disturbing Opal. When it came to human beings, Adrian didn't like many, but he liked Opal. She was everything he thought he might be one day, when he was 9 or 10 years old and still had some hope left in him. Brave. Smart. Funny. Tough. She hadn't let him see her cry once, even though he knew she'd been crying the second time he took her to the bathroom. Nor, he thought, did he ever expect to see her cry.

"So, Mr. Bad Guy," she asked him when he brought her back to the truck, "who's going to shoot me? You or Skinny Man?"

"Nobody's going to shoot you, kid," he said. "Don't be thinking that way. Your folks will pay the ransom and we'll turn you loose."

"What if they don't pay?"

"They'll pay, kid. Give it a rest."

"But, what if they don't?"

"Then this will all be a big waste of time, won't it? Now get in the truck."

"Are you going to shoot me if they don't pay?"

"Shut up, kid." He shut the door a little harder than he meant to, and felt bad.

A few minutes later, he brought her a peanut butter and jelly sandwich and her refilled Nalgene. "You worry too much, kid," he told her and gently closed the door.

But now she had him worried. He wondered about the end game. It wasn't as straightforward as he might like it. What would they do after they got the money? He had no doubt that the ransom would be delivered, but what then? Once they turned the girl loose, all bets were off. No more leverage and not much of a place to hide.

He looked at his watch. 4:30. Still two hours and a half to sunset by his calculation and it would be light enough to see until 8.

"I'm goin' for a walk," he said to Jack.

"Where the hell do you think you're going? You can't leave her here with me. What if she has to go to the bathroom again?"

"Then you'll just have to deal with it, won't you?" Adrian considered that and didn't like the possibilities that came to mind. "Besides, she just went. I'll be back soon."

He wanted to add, "Stay away from her," but he didn't.

As he walked by the Tahoe, he reached into his pocket, pushed the "lock" button on the remote entry key and looked to see if Jack might have noticed the click of the solenoids. The other man had laid back into one of the camp chairs, and his hat was pulled down over his eyes. Adrian knew he would be snoring in less than two minutes.

Adrian grabbed his pack and hiked up hill for half an hour until he came to the BLM road they had followed in. He knew the way out by the way they had come in, but what other options did he have? There had to be more than one way off this plateau.

He examined the roadbed and found several distinct tire marks overlaying the tracks of the Tahoe. He also noted how obvious their tracks into the side canyon were. He found a broken-off juniper branch and worked at erasing them to below the rim of the canyon, which took considerable time. Then he walked cross-country to a high, rocky point a quarter mile from the road, where he sat and scanned the country with his binoculars.

Way out to the north, he saw something glittering on the horizon, and he watched it intently, wondering what would cause that. After a bit, he realized it was a windmill. He pulled the Colorado atlas out of his pack, laid it open in his lap to the corresponding page and found the well on the map. It was 15 miles away. He examined the topography between himself and the windmill, noting roads and four-wheel-drive tracks that would take him there and then to a highway. He stuck a route in his mind and labeled it "back door." Then, he walked back to camp. Jack was still asleep.

Sleeping that much can't be good for your heart, Jack, Adrian thought, *and God forbid you should have a heart attack.* A grim little laugh came out of him, and Jack stirred in his chair.

Chapter Twenty-Four: A Kept Temper

B*efore the crew in Delta set out* for Cottonwood Campground, it was necessary to sort out who would ride with whom — an exercise in diplomacy. It would not do to have Joe or Kelly and Sabrina with Helen and Ross. So the father, son and son's girlfriend ended up in the back seat of the Tundra with Sara driving and Archer riding shotgun. Tom and Jesse rode in the back seat of the Explorer.

As Sara followed Ross, Archer began working on a thing in his lap to the light of his headlamp. Sara was not sure at first what it was, as it was wrapped in a light canvas bag, but soon recognized it as a crossbow.

"What are you doing?" she asked. Joe looked over Archer's shoulder, also curious.

"Figuring this thing out," he answered. "Please to keep your eyes on the road."

"Yessir, Mr. Bossman," she said. Archer grinned.

"Now?" said Joe.

"It seems like a good time. I might need it."

"Why not before?" Sara asked.

With a pair of needle-nose pliers, Archer strung a thin piece of stainless steel cable through a hole in one end of the bow. He put the bow between his legs. Using his thighs, he compressed it enough to wrap the cable several times around the notch in the other end and then tuck it under itself. When he let the pressure off, the cable went taut. He strummed it and it hummed a low key.

"Has your day been as full as mine, Ms. Cafferty?" he asked.

Sara sighed and hunched toward the steering wheel. "I believe so, Mr. MacClehan."

"Then you will understand why this has been delayed."

"Wasn't that thing hanging on your living room wall, AJ?" Joe asked

"Yep. This morning, it was a museum piece."

"Do you think it will work?"

With the butt of the weapon against his stomach, Archer pulled the cable back to the trigger catch. It took both hands, and out of the corner of her eye Sara saw the bicep in his left arm bulge. He didn't cock it, but let the pressure off slowly.

"It'll work."

"What are you going to do with it?" Kelly asked.

"I might just catch me a vulture," AJ answered, leaving the rest to wonder what he meant.

Sometime later, the Explorer and pickup slowed at the top of the grade into Cottonwood. Each let a passenger off without stopping and drove on. Archer and Tom waited for their eyes to adjust to the light of a quarter moon, then began a near-silent dogtrot alongside the rim road to the east. They stopped a half-hour out where the road veered south toward the rim and checked themselves against the quad map. They were half way to the side canyon. They rested and listened. Tom took a pair of night-vision binoculars out of his pack and scanned ahead. Nothing moving. After ten minutes, they went on.

Fifteen minutes later, a set of headlights appeared a few miles to the east. The two men kept moving, and watched the lights get closer and listened to the growl of the engine grow louder until it was just a few hundred yards away. About the time they were going to have to find a place to hide, the pickup turned hard left to the south, bounced across the plateau for a ways and then abruptly stopped out near the edge of the canyon. The lights went out. The motor switched off. Several seconds later, the sounds of country radio came wafting across the desert.

"Parked." Tom said in a low tone.

"In the middle of nowhere."

"They'll never hear us," Tom said, as George Strait sang clearly to them. "Amarillo by morning . . . "

By that time, Sara, Jesse and the rest of them were in Cottonwood Campground. Sara and Jesse helped Kelly and Sabrina get into their new tent. Joe took his pack and went out away from the rest.

Sara and Jesse set Tom's tent up and spread out the men's sleeping bags and then turned their attention to Sara's tent. A half-hour later, they were not much closer to getting to bed than they had been when they started. Sara was learning more about efficient tent design than she wanted to at midnight-thirty, and it was getting surly out.

"Have you ever put this thing up before?" Jesse asked.

"No." Sara was struggling to push the last shock pole through the sleeves of the tent. It was not going well. Her headlamp bobbed as she tried in vain to push the springy fiberglass shaft through the fabric tunnel. "No, I haven't."

"Give me that," Jesse said, and took the pole from Sara. "You're supposed to practice putting it up *before* you need it."

"First of all," Sara said, "I don't appreciate it when someone just takes something. . ."

"And second of all?" Jesse asked. She then used a word reserved in Sara's mind for stevedores and teenage boys, followed by a low growl.

"This thing is a piece of . . . "

"Second of all," Sara said, "getting angry is not going to solve the problem."

"Coming from the temper queen, that's pretty profound." And, there was that word again.

Sara froze then, and Jesse felt it when she did.

Dammit, Jesse thought, *I have a big mouth. Of course, I should have. My foot's often in it.*

"Sara, I'm sorry," she blurted.

Sara came back to life. "Jesse," she said carefully, "being a bitch doesn't suit you, so kindly quit it. May I?" She took the pole from Jesse, and began again trying to thread it through the sleeves that were supposed to suspend the tent from its flexible frame.

Jesse stood silent and watched her. She wasn't exactly sure how she felt about what had just happened between them, but she knew she was surprised.

After a moment's careful struggle, Sara managed it.

"There!" she said through clenched teeth. "Holy Samoley! What a piece of . . . "

"Careful." Jesse laughed. "Wow. That was interesting."

Sara sighed. She was near exhausted and running shorter on patience than she liked. "How so?" She set the final shock pole into its last socket, and the tent billowed into the resemblance of a shelter.

"Where's the fly, please." she said.

Jesse picked up the fly and flung it over the tent like a bed-sheet over a mattress, and the two of them went about securing it to the tent.

"I have no clue how you managed to hold your temper there. Aren't you the same girl who once tried to filet a certain guy we both know for not letting her have her way?"

Sara was ready for sleep. "C'mon," she said, "get your bag in the stupid tent and let's get to bed."

"You can go to sleep with AJ and Tom out there?"

"Somebody has to," Sara climbed into the tent with her bag and a pillow. "I'm going to try anyway. I don't know about you, but I've been up for 20 hours

— no, longer — and it's been one hell of a day. Tomorrow — today — is going to be another one. Bed!"

"Bossy!"

"Grabby!" Sara started giggling. Jesse joined her first in the giggling and then in the tent. A few minutes later, they were both in their sleeping bags.

After a while, Jesse asked quietly, "So, what ever did happen to that girl who had to have her way?"

From deep in her bag, Sara said, "She turned into a psychopath and started killing nosy noisy tent-mates."

"G'night, then, Ms. Psycho."

"Grrrr."

Sara was asleep before Jesse, but Jesse had the conundrum in the bag next to hers to consider.

Chapter Twenty-Five: A Walk In The Dark

J*esse's consternation at Sara's self-control* was considerable — and deservedly so. In other times and places before and during the Great Grizzly Adventure — upon which Sara met Tom, Jesse and Archer — Sara had been possessed of a wondrous and terrible temper with which she had increasingly often tried to bully others into doing what she wanted. Once, she tried throwing it at Archer and had it flung back at her. That had never happened before, and it both surprised and galvanized her. It was the beginning of a coming of age, for she had already recognized the destructive nature of her anger upon relationships and was struggling to control it.

At the end of the Adventure, she had gone back to her world — where Archer and his friends would never live

— knowing that she was unprepared to live in theirs. At least not yet. She took with her indelible memories of four days in the wilderness and a close encounter of the bear kind.

If someone wanted to know what a griz smelled like and what it was like to straddle one, they might ask Sara and she could tell them.

If some of the grizzly rubbed off on her, it also took something away from her, and that was her willingness to be angry. At some microsecond in that encounter, Sara Cafferty lost her temper in the most profound of ways. It dropped out of her through her right hand as she used it to try to twist a bear's ear off.

She would always remember the exact moment. A dead calm overtook her in the midst of the brief battle — it was only seconds long. She still had a grip on the critter's hide and it had risen to its hind legs. Over the bear's shoulder, Skyrocket Ridge rose in the background. Jesse and Tom stood frozen at the edge of the meadow. Archer had risen to *his* hind legs, and he was looking right at her. There was something in his eyes she would never forget and never wanted to see again: utter rage, she thought, but not her kind of rage; not red-hot, erupting, uncontrolled rage, but ice-blue, cold, deliberate, incredibly dangerous anger. That was when she thought she lost hers, for it was gone the next time she went looking for it a few weeks later in Los Angeles traffic when someone cut her off. Given the perspective from a bear's back she had let it go, for it was apparent that all that was important was right before her at that moment, and if she could survive this last tantrum, she would never have reason to be uncontrollably angry again.

Perhaps that's why Sara growled at Jesse, from the bearness that had rubbed off on her when she finally, really lost her temper.

About the time Jesse was contemplating Sara's loss, Tom and Archer came to where the road swung out around the head of the arroyo where Sara suspected the kidnappers and Opal might be. Watching the right side of the road for tracks, they walked quickly along the trace. It was Tom who saw the anomaly in the ridge along the right tread marking where something had turned off the main road. A faint track but no fresh tread marks ran out toward the head of the arroyo.

All was still except for occasional snatches of John Prine. Tom scanned the plateau for any sign of another human, and, with the exception of the pickup — a third-mile away on the canyon edge — there was nothing. It was apparent that whoever was in the pickup out on the rim was oblivious to their presence, or anything outside the cab, for that matter. They moved cautiously through the sage and rabbit brush along each side of the track — so their own footprints weren't obvious — until the arroyo opened and the trace dropped into it. They stopped instinctively and stood quiet listening as Tom scanned forward. Archer closed his eyes and felt into the darkness. One minute grew into five.

Archer hunkered down beside the left track feeling like they were getting nowhere. Nothing had been proved or disproved. A broken juniper branch lay in the trace, and Archer reached down and picked it up. Small as it was, it seemed to be blocking the way. He laid it to the side. In the moonlight, he could see a small anomaly in the surface of the dirt. He tapped Tom's leg to get his attention, then put his back to the pickup and took his headlamp off, held it close to the ground and turned the red LED on. There in the dust was a tiny portion of a fresh boot track.

Tom held up a palm flat to Archer and then moved silently into the canyon. Archer watched him out of sight. Against the backdrop of the pure silence of the place Tim McGraw's faint voice reached out.

Archer drew himself into a cross-legged position beside a big sage, the position he had held in the beginning of his morning dream — *What, 18 hours ago?* he thought — and the elements of the day and the dream began sorting in his mind.

In another 18 hours, the kidnappers would have both the money and Opal, and all the moves appeared to be theirs for the 24 after that. He slowly drew out his thoughts about them. There were at least three kidnappers — two vultures and a coral snake. He felt instinctively that one of them, most likely the snake, was someone who knew the family on intimate terms. It was the only way the kidnappers could know where Opal was at a given moment, especially at the moment she was taken. Someone had foreknowledge of Opal and Ross's hike, where it would go and when.

He ran through the list of people he knew who would have that knowledge, as well as the list of those who might. It was short. Helen, of course, and Ross. Maybe Kelly and maybe Sabrina. A remote possibility in Joe.

So who would communicate the information to the kidnappers? He automatically sorted out Helen and Kelly. Definitely not Joe. Ross? What did he have to gain by such an act? What was the relationship between him and Opal? Good? Bad?

And what about Sabrina? She was certainly beautiful, but was she poisonous?

His mind was drawn back to the dream, particularly the coral snake. It switched on and off abruptly and Opal followed its lead with complete trust, even as she ran away from him. Its resemblance to a holograph stuck in his mind, and he let it settle there and watched for thoughts to rise around it. Not real. Holographic. Virtual. It was a broadcast maybe, or some other kind of electronic phenomena. Computerized? Communication.

Cell phone.

Maybe there was a player who was a phone buddy of Opal's.

He thought about the image of Sara chasing Opal — and the snake. He didn't wish to involve her on that level. It seemed too dangerous, and if there was anything he didn't want to do it was endanger Sara. But he also remembered his knowledge and experience of the dreams. They must be gone into or disaster ensues.

Another thought stirred then, one about disclosure, and he nearly automatically dismissed it, but it stuck with him. *She needs to know her part in things,* something told him. He reserved judgment about that for the moment and reached farther into the dream. "Broken hearts don't heal in the dark," he heard Five Bears say.

What does that mean, he wondered, *and whose heart is broken, here, anyway?*

As if in answer to that question, the pickup's occupants turned up the volume out on the edge of the canyon and Patsy Cline's clear contralto came two-stepping across the plateau. "I go out walkin,' after midnight . . ."

Miranda Kaye Starr's image rose before him then, as it did from time to time, and he felt as he always did when he saw her clearly, even after all these years: bereft, shattered and alone. He knew the answer then, and he did not like it one damned bit.

He knew instinctively that healing a broken heart meant having to expose it. He also knew his heart was encased in some sort of stone. He purposely kept it that way, but if there was a person on the planet who'd found a crack in the encasement, it was Sara Cafferty. She'd planted herself there the summer before like a young ponderosa seedling in a niche in granite. He hadn't watered it much, but he couldn't bring himself to pull the seedling out. A fracture in the encasement seemed to be forming, and he would have to let it run its course if his heart was to heal. But that might mean an incredible amount of pain. He wondered if he was brave enough to face it.

Something moved close by and Archer shook Miranda's phantom and the reality of Sara out of his head. A second later, Tom squatted beside him.

"Sara's right," he whispered. "Tracks in. None out."

Soon they were trotting back the way they had come. It was near two o'clock when they moved past the musical pickup, and past three when they came to camp. They were grateful to find Tom's tent up and their bags rolled out, and they turned in without ceremony. Archer shut down his mind, which had been planning the coming day since they began back toward camp. There would not be much sleep this night, but it was better to have a little than none at all. It was, Archer knew, going to be one hell of a day for all concerned.

Chapter Twenty-Six: We Can't Fail

Archer awoke and lay in the tent for a few minutes, remembering the night before and thinking about the details of the coming day. They would deliver the money in the afternoon and then would begin a waiting game that nobody in his estimation knew quite how to play.

He looked at his watch. It was 7 a.m. "Sevlakovs," he said quietly.

"Yo," answered the other side of the tent.

"Go wake Jesse . . ." He hesitated.

"And the redhead?" Tom asked.

"Yes," Archer said. "The redhead, too."

When Tom was out of the tent, Archer considered his idea of the night before, the one about disclosure. To one extent, the idea of sharing his dreams with others felt liberating. The dreams often seemed a huge burden. But what if it was too heavy for the others to bear? Then what? He had carried the dreams since he was 10 and younger. His mother understood because she had them too. Tom was at least as strong as he, and he didn't really carry them as much as analyze them. The three of them were evidently capable, but did he have the right to burden others? Would it reshape their relationships? And how much?

A memory came to him of something Miranda had once said to him. They were fighting about one of the few things they ever fought about, her distress that he often tried to keep troubles to himself. They were a ways from being married, but both knew they were headed in that direction. Mira, in her inimitable style, had been studying up on it. She invoked what she called the Rule of For Better or Worse. "When you're selfish with your burdens, AJ, it makes me wonder if you're going to be selfish with your blessings, too."

She'd been right, but good Western American male that he was, it took him a while to learn to trust her with his fears and defeats as well as his joys and successes. She was good at sniffing them out though, and it got to a place where when she asked, "Anything wrong?" he was not ashamed to say what might be on his mind.

Miranda knew about the dreams. She had to in Archer's estimation. They were as much a part of him as archery and airplanes. If he was to water that seedling rooted in the encasement around his heart, he would have to tell Sara, too.

With these thoughts chasing each other around in his head, he crawled out into the morning. After orienting himself — he'd not seen the place in the light before, at least not from the ground — he went to the picnic table that held the stove and dug around and found makings for coffee.

Tom showed up a minute later. A few minutes after that, Sara and Jesse appeared, like sisters crawling from a shared tent. The reality of Sara struck at Archer like small lightning bolts. Even with a bad case of pillow head, she glowed from days in the outdoors, as beautiful as sunlight.

She gave him a sleepy smile, and he answered with his crooked grin. Something stirred within the encasement.

Maybe, he thought. *Maybe.*

Jesse stepped up to the table. "Well?" she asked.

"Sara appears to be right," Tom said.

"They are in that canyon, then," said Sara.

"Tom found tracks in but none out," Archer said, "and someone went to a lot of trouble to cover their trail above the rim of the side canyon."

He poured them each a cup of coffee and motioned them to sit. "In a few minutes, the others will be up, but there's something I want to talk about first." He took a seat next to Sara and across from Jesse. Tom brought his cup to the table and sat opposite Sara.

The thought of "team" again welled up in Archer, and that other thought about disclosure followed it into view. He sat quietly. His hands found their way together, palms facing, fingertips together with his index fingers against his lips — a prayerful gesture that seemed to seal his mouth. This had been an unconscious gesture, but he took note of it and it gave him pause.

One risk, he thought, *is that one or both will think I'm crazy. Another is that Sara is not going to be part of the team, and it's just my wishful thinking that makes it seem so.*

He looked at Jesse and then at Tom. He could feel Sara sitting quietly next to him. By telling Sara, he realized, he could tell Jesse. Why that was so, he wasn't sure, but it felt oddly right. He was getting used to the idea, anyway, but he worried that he was being premature. What if this was delusion?

Archer MacClehan didn't suffer doubt inordinately, but he had learned to pay attention when he did. Something wasn't setting quite right, and he wanted to know why it wasn't. That might take time. With the rest of them looking at him expectantly, though, he had to say something.

"First of all," Archer said, "I think someone with ties to the family is feeding information to the bad guys. It's the only way that someone would know where Opal was well enough to kidnap her. To complicate matters, I think it might be Opal herself. I suspect she's got a phone buddy who's either one of the kidnappers or an accomplice."

"That might work someplace else," Jesse said, "but cell phones don't appear to work in this canyon. Mine sure doesn't."

"Texting works," Sara said. "Put in a text and hit 'Send,' and a minute later — sometimes longer — it goes out. Same on receiving. It's not instant, but incoming texts arrive. Hard to tell what the delay is, but I'd guess consistently less than five minutes."

"So," Jesse said, "you think Opal has been telling a friend about where she is, and that person is passing it on? Some friend."

"If that's the case," said Tom slowly — he sighed, "whoever they are, they probably don't plan to let Opal live."

It got very quiet at the table, with the elephant in the room now sitting in the center of the table where everyone could see it. It was a thought that had crossed each mind but was never spoken until now.

"Then it's going to be up to us to extract her." Sara said it and it surprised even her. The rest of the table was not exactly gaping at her, but she had their attention.

"Or we could call the FBI," said Tom.

"Do you really think we should?" Jesse asked.

Tom was not quick to answer. He looked around at the canyon surrounding them. It was his first real view of the place, having arrived in the dark the night before.

"That idea is more about absolution of responsibility than anything else," he finally said. "This is a heavy load we're lifting, and I am feeling it. I will bow to your opinion, Captain."

"We know what they promised to do if we get the police involved," Archer said, "and the family has not agreed to it. If we do involve law enforcement, they would have to stay far away from here and act more as a net to catch the kidnappers after we get Opal back. And even that would have to be pretty subtle. Tom and I were up on the plateau last night, and believe me, there are too many places a person can hide and watch from to think the kidnappers wouldn't know if the FBI or state police descended en masse."

"So," Jesse said, "what do you think of our chances of getting the girl back alive?"

"Opal," said Archer, "Her name is Opal." Amidst hovering images of her freckled face and funny grin, the dream coursed through his mind. He looked at his hands lying on the table in front of him and took a deep breath. He let it out slowly.

“Good,” he said. “I think our chances are very good.”

“And if we fail?” Tom said.

“We can’t fail,” Sara said.

“What do you mean, ‘can’t’?” Tom asked.

We can’t allow ourselves to think we’ll fail,” Jesse said.

“Yes,” said Sara, “that’s what I mean.” But what she really meant was that for some reason she knew they were not to fail, that Something-Or-Other was at work here or they would not all be sitting at this table. At the same time she knew that the thought might be delusional, but for everyone, it would be better to believe than to doubt.

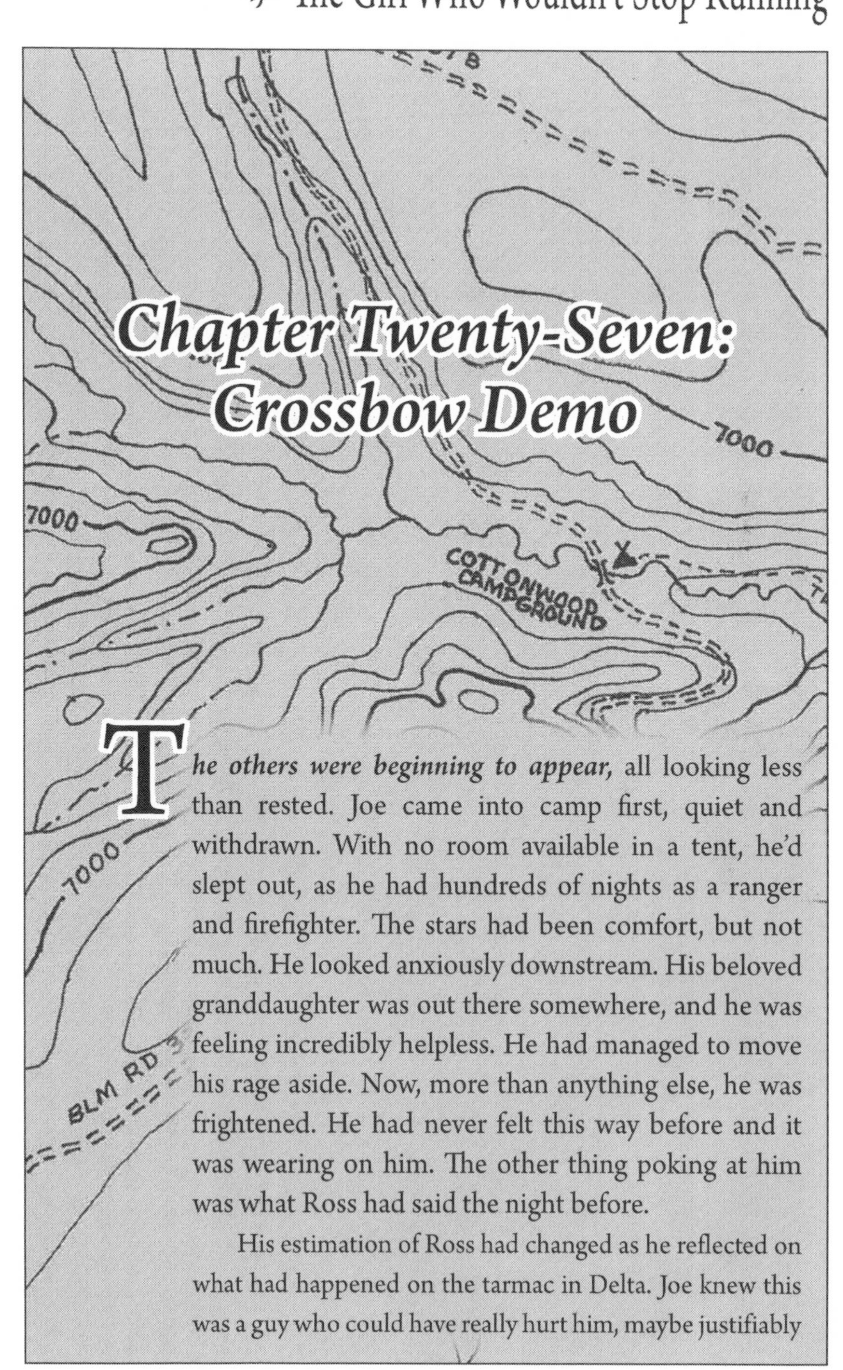

Chapter Twenty-Seven: Crossbow Demo

The others were beginning to appear, all looking less than rested. Joe came into camp first, quiet and withdrawn. With no room available in a tent, he'd slept out, as he had hundreds of nights as a ranger and firefighter. The stars had been comfort, but not much. He looked anxiously downstream. His beloved granddaughter was out there somewhere, and he was feeling incredibly helpless. He had managed to move his rage aside. Now, more than anything else, he was frightened. He had never felt this way before and it was wearing on him. The other thing poking at him was what Ross had said the night before.

His estimation of Ross had changed as he reflected on what had happened on the tarmac in Delta. Joe knew this was a guy who could have really hurt him, maybe justifiably so, but chose not to. He also seemed to care very deeply for Opal, enough to understand that she didn't like him and yet be genuinely fond of her.

Joe watched his son and his girlfriend emerge from their tent. Kelly looked lost and reasonably so. He hadn't looked Joe in the eye or hardly acknowledged him since he had arrived in Delta, but something about Sabrina gave Joe pause. Her calm presence seemed to be holding Kelly in place. It was as if she was disconnected from the angst of the situation and anchored to something else.

Helen looked worst of all, and Joe's heart suddenly went out to her. He had liked Helen immediately when Kelly brought her home from college years before, and he was remembering why. She'd been a great person before the divorce, and Joe was now cognizant that had not changed. Even in her current state, Helen was still the Helen he had admired before her marriage to his son went south. And she still trusted him. He's the one she'd called when she didn't know who else to call. So, if she hadn't changed and he hadn't changed, who had?

"Maybe you should get your son in a corner, sometime . . . " echoed through his mind.

Archer's red pack sat on a picnic table near Sara's pick-up. Archer was sitting near it, fooling with the crossbow again. Joe walked to the table.

"You going to take that?" he asked.

"Yep," Archer answered, and held it up in the sighting position. The crossbow wasn't very big, Joe realized. It featured a lithe-looking metal bow just 18 inches long. The stock, made of hardwood, was a bit longer, with a pistol-type butt and a trigger mounted in the commensurate spot. The play on the bowstring looked to be just over five inches.

"Not a very long-range weapon," Joe said.

"Depends on whose using it for what, I'd guess," Archer answered.

"How's that thing cock?"

"I finally figured it out," Archer said. "Someone spent some time thinking this thing out."

He gripped the stock at the front, directly under the cross piece, and pulled down. The wooden frame pulled away to reveal a piece of one-inch steel channel, to which the bow itself was welded. The wooden piece swiveled just in front of the trigger, revealing a decorative curve in the stock to be a seam. As the traveling piece of stock came to an angle of 120 degrees with the steel channel, there was a click, and Archer reversed course.

The piece in his hand now levered a three-quarter-inch thick lamination of wood and steel up from the channel. Its free end was notched toward the back of the stock and after about an inch of travel, it caught the bowstring. As Archer pushed the stock back into place, the traveling piece pushed the string, bending the bow. When the string passed the trigger stop, Archer used the back of a finger to push the trigger forward, and the double catch popped up into place. Letting off pressure on the stock allowed the string to come to rest against the catch.

Archer then pulled the stock back toward himself an inch, and the piece in the middle, relieved of the pressure of the bowstring, settled back into the channel to become the receptacle for the bolt.

Sara, Tom, Jesse and Ross joined Joe in watching Archer demonstrate the crossbow.

"Amazing," Ross said.

"Somebody did some heavy engineering on this thing," Archer said appreciatively.

"But can you hit anything with it?" Joe asked.

"I guess we'll see," Archer said. He pulled a bright green bolt out of the canvas bag and set it against the bowstring. He looked for a suitable target. He didn't necessarily want to lose a bolt on first shot and he didn't wish to imbed the bolt in a live tree. There was, however, a ponderosa stump about 40 yards away, right near the trailhead sign. Archer made sure the area was clear and then pointed the crossbow toward the stump.

All he knew of archery ran into his right arm and hand, including the relative strength of the bow, the weight of the bolt and even small considerations for altitude and wind, which would make negligible difference at this range with this weapon. He didn't consciously aim but saw the bolt flying to the target. He squeezed the trigger.

With a distinctive and resonant "twunk," a green lightning bolt leapt off the crossbow and flew nearly dead center into the stump. No one watching — Joe, Jesse, Sara, Tom nor Ross — was quite sure which made the sound, the release or the landing.

Everyone stared first at the green bolt imbedded in the stump. Then nearly as one, they turned their attention back to Archer. Everyone but Tom and Jesse had their mouth open.

"Holy . . . " said Ross.

"Samoley," Sara finished for him.

Archer looked up from the crossbow at the group staring at him and started laughing. "Seems to work pretty good," he said, "although it feels like it pulls a little to the right."

He got up and walked to the stump with the rest of the group right behind him. He grabbed the bolt and pulled. It was driven in hard.

"Tom?" he said.

Tom grabbed the bolt and gave it a tentative tug. Then he gripped it with both hands and put a boot against the stump. His arms swelled with effort, but finally and with a bit of wiggling, the 12-inch bolt came out of the wood.

"What the hell is that made of?" Joe asked.

Archer gave a rueful smile. "Push rod out of a '69 Ford 302. Something I thought I might rebuild someday. Now I'm a half-dozen parts short."

Chapter Twenty-Eight: The Anger Meter

Archer grunted as he hefted his pack, full of two million dollars. "What did you say this weighs, greenhorn?" he asked.

"Greenhorn first class, to you, Mr. MacClehan," Sara retorted. "You promoted me yourself, remember. The money weighs 59 pounds, give or take a few ounces."

"Sixty-four with the pack. OK."

"What do you mean, 'OK?' "

He hefted the pack and swung it onto his back, let it settle and took a few steps. "Just checking to see if Tom's knees will take the strain," Archer said.

What he was really thinking of was the scene in the dream in which he threw his pack at the vulture. He knew he couldn't pitch that weight far, but he also knew that the dreams were often symbolic rather than literal. Throwing his pack at the vulture might not look exactly like it had in the dream. Time would tell.

"I thought you and Ross would be delivering the money," Sara said.

"Tom's going," Archer said. He lowered the pack back onto the picnic table where Tom and Jesse were poring over a quad map. "Sara," he said, "would you bring Ross to join us, please?"

Sara was surprised by the assignment, but went willingly to the other side of the campground, where Ross and Helen's tent sat near the stream. She found them sitting at a picnic table of their own. They were, as might be expected, looking worse for wear this morning.

"Archer would like to talk to you, Ross."

"Archer?" Ross said, as if searching for a reference.

Sara realized not many people called Archer by his proper name. "AJ," she said, "Joe's friend who flew him down from Montana."

"About?"

"We are going over maps and he wants your input."

"Alright. I'll be there in a minute."

Sara didn't move, nor did she say anything. She stood expectantly waiting. Ross looked at her in surprise. "I guess you mean now," he said.

"Yes, please," Sara said.

"I'll be right back, Helen," he said.

Helen looked up at the sound of her name, and Sara could see that she was still as vacant as she'd been the night before. *Maybe Ross is just trying to keep her from floating away altogether,* she thought.

"I'll stay with Helen if you'd like," she said.

"Thank you. That would be good." He slid off the bench and moved stiffly away. Sara took his place at the table. They sat in silence for a while and then a question occurred to Sara.

"Helen," she said, "does Opal have a cell phone?"

Helen didn't look at Sara when she answered, which sounded as if she was 100 miles away. "Yes. Of course she does. Everybody has a cell phone these days."

"What's her phone number?"

Helen thought for a minute. "206-888-2220."

Sara brought out a pen and the small notebook she carried for stray notes about rocks and wrote down the number. "Did she take it with her on the hike yesterday?"

"Of course she did. She never goes anyplace without it."

"Do you know her password for voicemail?"

"Why?"

Sara considered her answer. How important was it to know this? Would telling Helen about Archer's theory make things worse or better? She decided that if Archer was right, knowing the password could make things infinitely better. It could save Opal's life. "Archer thinks someone who knows her, maybe a phone buddy of hers, might be feeding information to the kidnappers."

Helen looked at her in disbelief. Sara saw some sort of spark move behind her eyes. "Who would do that? Why would anybody do such a thing?

"Money can make people do some terrible things, Helen," she said gently.

Helen looked off in the direction of the tent Kelly and Sabrina shared.

"You're right," she said. "Yes, it will." Helen chewed on her lower lip.

"Her password is either 'Alice' or 'Smokey,' like the bear. Those are her passwords for everything."

"You're certain."

Helen looked at Sara full on. She seemed fully present for the first time since Sara had met her. "I'm her mother. I'm certain."

"How you doin', Helen?" Sara asked.

"Not so great, to tell you the truth," Helen said.

"I can believe that."

"What's your name?" Helen asked.

"Sara. Sara Cafferty."

"You're a friend of AJ's"

"Archer's. Yes."

"Do you have kids, Sara?" Helen asked.

"No. No, I don't," Sara admitted.

"Don't ever have kids, Sara," Helen said. "Never."

"We'll see about that, I imagine," Sara said. "Tell me about Opal."

Helen looked down the canyon and took a deep breath.

"Well," she began, "first of all, she's thirteen and she's really smart." She looked back at Sara. "And if she gets away from whoever took her, they will never ever catch her."

"Why do you say that?"

"Because she can outrun anybody. At least anybody I know."

"She's really fast?"

"Fast and endurant. She's already got a couple of cross-country records that will probably stand forever."

"And she loves it."

Helen looked at Sara in surprise. "How do you know that?"

"If you don't love it, you don't get cross country records very often."

"Do you have cross country records, Sara?"

Sara gave a short laugh. "Yep. A few."

Jesse came across the camp ground and slid onto the bench next to Sara.

"AJ wants to see you," she said. "I'll hang out here for a bit."

Sara reached across the table and took Helen's hand in hers. "We're going to get Opal back, Helen," she said, "and she'll be fine."

"How can you know that?" Helen asked. Jesse asked the same question with her eyes.

"I just know," Sara said, and went to join the others.

The others were looking at Sara with some expectation when she arrived. Archer, Tom, Ross and Kelly had a map stretched out on the table. "Have you ever been out here?" Archer asked. He pointed to the trailhead downstream of the kidnappers' canyon.

"Yes. A couple of times I've used that trail to get into the canyon. Some very interesting aggregate along the way."

"We want to create a diversion, and a relatively spectacular one."

"What's the plan?"

With his finger tracing a route on the map, Archer said, "You, Jesse and Sabrina go to this trailhead and then hike back to camp here, being as silly, loud and, um, sexy as possible, including splashing around in the creek right about here for 20 minutes."

"Yes. I would help do that, but to what end."

"It could be risky," Tom said.

"How risky?"

"It's pretty likely that the bad guys have guns," Tom said.

Sara moved two jumps into the seriousness of the situation. "Of course they do."

"That's how risky," Tom said.

"What did Jesse say?"

"I said I'd go." Jesse had come quietly back to the table.

"Who's with Helen?" Ross asked.

"Joe's sitting with her," Jesse said.

"Joe?" Kelly was concerned.

"They're fine, Kelly. Just fine," Jesse said.

Kelly was somewhat nervous about that. He'd always known the details of his actions leading up to the divorce might become known to his dad someday, and that all hell would then break loose. He had experienced his father's temper. He'd always imagined that it would be a long-distance confrontation, one mitigated by the 600 miles between his growing-up home in Montana and his new one on the Olympic Peninsula. Now piled upon his concern for Opal was the worry that Helen and his dad were reconnecting. This might allow his dad to see things in a much different light than Kelly had presented the situation in when the marriage imploded.

As Kelly ruminated on that, Sara leaned over the map and put her finger on the place where Archer had suggested they splash around in the creek, just a bit downstream of the outlet to the kidnappers' canyon. She looked up at Jesse to find her looking right at her.

"I can do that," she said, "but why are we doing it?"

Everyone was looking at Archer. "To create a diversion while I come down this crack," — he traced a narrow slot dropping from the canyon wall into the creek with his index finger — "and get into position right here."

Sara looked at his finger on the map and compared it to hers. Archer's position appeared to her to be very exposed, particularly to someone walking the trail below the boulder field, a route the kidnappers had to take to get to the money. She pulled her finger off the map and stood back.

"How is endangering yourself going to help save Opal?" she said.

Archer was nonplus for an answer. He couldn't tell her about the dream — not yet, not with Ross, Kelly and Sabrina at the table with the four of them.

Sara looked at Archer expectantly, waiting for an answer. He was slow to answer, and it was finally Tom that spoke up.

"Someone needs to be on the ground in the canyon if we are going to get Opal out of there. Archer's the one who has the skills to get in without being detected."

Jesse looked at Tom in surprise. He opened his hands in supplication, apologizing silently for the white lie. The three of them knew that there was another person at that table who was much more qualified for that sort of action. What Jesse couldn't know was what the dream dictated. It was Archer, not Tom, who was to be waiting for the vultures.

"That doesn't make sense," Sara said. "Show me how logic dictates that's true."

It got very quiet at the table. Even Jesse had no idea of what to say to that.

"Archer?" Sara said.

He looked at the rim of the canyon above their heads as he answered. "Sometimes logic is not all we have to work with, Sara."

"You want to give me an example?" For the first time in a long time, Sara could feel the anger meter climbing above the blue zone and into the orange, which surprised her and even frightened her a bit.

Now is not the time to lose your temper, she told herself, but there was something pushing the needle to the right.

"I'm sorry, I can't."

"You're sorry? You'll be really sorry if you end up dead!" The anger meter was still climbing, and her fear of it pegging out grabbed her by the back of the neck, pushed her away from the picnic table and flung her off toward Opal's boulder.

Chapter Twenty-Nine: Sara's Rock

S*ara's abrupt departure caused things to get* very quiet at the table. Archer looked after her and said quietly, "Jess? Will you go talk to her, please? It's important that we get underway."

"Yessir," she said. She sighed and swung away from the table. A minute later she caught up with Sara, who was unknowingly emulating Opal, tossing rocks off the top of the big boulder into the pool at its base.

Jesse climbed to the top and sat cross-legged next to her friend. She heard that word, "friend," in her mind, in fact, and knew it was the right one. There was some small part of her that did not want to like this beautiful woman next to her at all, the same jealous bone that got her in more trouble than she could get completely out of long ago, when she first met and came to love Archer MacClehan. She told it firmly to shut up.

Sara finally looked at Jesse sitting next to her. "Is there something wrong with me, Jesse? Some fatal flaw I can't see? I mean, what was that about?"

Jesse looked at her hands.

"Look, Jess. I know you love that . . . that . . . "

"Idiot?"

"He's not an idiot!" Sara said it with such an inflection that Jesse winced. The girl had it bad, she knew. No cure excepting total abstinence. She considered suggesting it just long enough to grow a grim little smile.

"What?" Sara asked, and the smile disappeared.

"And you love him, too," Jesse said. "But you don't know all there is to know about Archer MacClehan." She smiled ruefully. "And neither do I, though I know more than you surely, since I've known him about 12 times longer than you; 14 years to your 14 months. And I've loved him about 12 times longer than you, too. The difference is that he has loved you about 12 times longer than he has loved me."

"What do you mean, 'loved you?' " Sara said.

"Whether you and he know it or not," Jesse said, "that guy loves you." She paused. "He loves me too, has for a long time — like a sister, dammit and 'Thank you, God,' at the same time. Whatever he's waitin' for ain't in me, evidently, for I have tried and cried and waited and even hated him — or tried to. But he's a hard man to hate, and you are a hard woman to hate, Sara. But if I didn't like you so much, I would hate your guts."

Jesse gave a grim little laugh. "Not that I haven't tried, you understand."

Sara put a hand on Jesse's shoulder and Jesse shook it off.

"Don't!" It came out of her like a shot. "This is hard enough!"

Sara went to stand and Jesse stopped her with a hand held up.

"Just stay right there," she said softly. "Just sit and listen and I, who like you too much to hate your guts, will spill mine; and you, who like me enough to forgive me wanting to hate your guts, will learn something about Archer and why he is how he is.

"It's not that AJ doesn't love me — or you. AJ would die for me, need be. He would die for Tom." Jesse looked toward camp. "He would — and might yet — die for Opal."

Sara shivered at the thought.

"But he *demonstrated* that he would die for you in that meadow along Skyrocket Creek last summer. And you — you crazy wench — demonstrated that same day that you would die for him. Which is one of the reasons I care enough to tell you these things."

She looked down the canyon. "When I met Archer, he was deeply in love with a girl named Miranda Starr, his high-school sweetheart. When he got out of the Academy, they got married. On their honeymoon, she was killed."

Sara let out a small moan.

"After that happened, Archer went crazy. Even I don't know quite how crazy, because he doesn't talk about it. Only one person in the world knows completely what happened in the ensuing four years."

"Tom," Sara said.

"Tom," confirmed Jesse, "and he ain't talkin', either."

"So, this happened how long ago? Fifteen, 16 years? And he's still mourning?"

Jesse looked surprised. "I wouldn't say he was mourning. He has yet to do that, and that is why he is stuck where he's stuck. And it was not nearly that long ago."

"I can do math," Sara pointed out. "You say you've known him 14 years. How long before you met him did Miranda die?"

"Miranda died three years and 11 months after I met AJ at the Academy."

"The Academy."

Jesse laughed ruefully. "The Air Force Academy. I was a doolie during his sophomore year at Colorado Springs."

"A doolie?"

"That's what incoming freshmen are called at the Academy."

"A doolie." Sara chewed on that for a while and Jesse waited while she chewed.

In the midst of that doolie year, and "out of the wild blue yonder," Archer liked to tease, Jesse Turnbull leveraged her way into what she percieved as an exclusive boys' club whose members were AJ and Tom. She figured these boys needed a girl in their club and maybe they did, even though the truth of the matter was that they were pretty efficient as just the two of them. Then things got sideways and messy. Jesse fell in love with the lead dog.

"Bad dog," Sara Cafferty might have said, had she known Jesse and Archer then. Not because Jesse didn't have a right to fall in love with Archer, but because at that time in Archer's life Sara would have recognized him as completely unavailable. He was in love with Miranda, and try as Jesse might, there was no changing that. After Miranda's death, Archer wasn't interested in an intimate involvement with anybody.

After somewhat more than a decade of sorting that out, Archer, Tom and Jesse lived in peace with each other and certain seemingly inalterable facts. Jesse loved Archer fiercely. Archer loved Jesse like a sister. They had accepted that there was nothing they could do about the disparity of affection between them, and they lived with it by practicing acceptance and compassion in their relationship. Implicitly, Jesse agreed not to push herself on Archer or expect him to change how he felt, and Archer agreed not to run away from her affection or feel guilty for not feeling about her the way she did about him.

It had been a hard agreement to come to, made over a series of incursions into and out of each other's lives. It became a good arrangement, though somewhat harder on Jesse than the others. Even yet, she might get caught up in hopefulness and hopelessness when it came to her deepest feelings for Archer. They both loved Tom as their dearest brother.

Finally Sara said, "I don't understand how you both went to the Academy — Archer would have graduated, what, 10 years ago? — yet neither of you are in the Air Force."

"Or the Reserves," concluded Jesse. "I quit after my third year— or more accurately, was asked to resign from the Academy — and then suffered a couple of years as an airman 'til my debt was paid, you might say. Archer was discharged five years after I left Colorado Springs, well after he began climbing out of his craziness. Maybe that's why the powers that be were kind."

Jessie paused, surprised that she had finally come to that conclusion and also somewhat pleased. It felt like taking a heavy pack off after a long hike.

"His was a medical discharge," she continued. "It could well have been . . ."

Jesse shut her mouth.

"Dishonorable." Sara finished her thought.

"Yes," Jesse said, "though I really doubt that he ever was."

Jesse was wrong to doubt.

In the years following Miranda's MacClehan's death, Archer did a number of dishonorable things. Jesse was aware of some of these actions; she just couldn't bring herself to judge Archer, much less condemn him for them. She had been in a very similar fight with herself, the one that had washed her out of the Academy.

She had watched him resurface — the only word she could use to describe his return from hell — and begin swimming against the current of previous actions. She knew something of his recovery but couldn't comprehend all of it, because she could not really know all that he had lost.

"I've seen him make these decisions before, Sara — the seemingly illogical ones. I happen to know that Tom is more able to do what AJ is proposing than AJ. But they have a secret — many secrets, in fact — that I'm not privy to. Even so, over these 14 years, I've learned to trust them both implicitly."

"We three have gotten into some crazy situations, and those two have been in many more," Jesse said. She looked back at camp. "It always works out. The circumstances by which you came into our lives is good proof of that. And now, here you are again."

Sara had listened to all of that in silence, and now remained so.

"So, there's really nothing wrong with you, Sara, except being beautiful and smart and a pain in the rear from time to time."

Sara sighed. "There's something else, Jess," she said. "This morning is the first time I've come close to losing my temper since the day we fought the bear. Nothing has made me angry since. I don't want to go back there."

"Then don't."

"Easy for you to say."

"Remember what triggered your last fit on that trip."

"Not counting the bear?"

"Not counting the bear."

"Crossing the ledge in the canyon."

"No. The thought of crossing the ledge in the canyon. You were scared."

Sara laughed at the memory. "Only somewhat petrified."

"And now you're scared something might happen to AJ."

Sara bit her lip, and a tear came to the corner of her left eye. "Only somewhat petrified." The tear jumped onto her cheek.

"Remember the rock?"

"Oh, yes." Sara could feel it in her hands.

"Maybe its time to find a big rock."

Sara patted their mutual seat and gave Jesse a teary smile. "This one might be big enough."

Jesse laughed. "Might be. But, remember that other rock, too. The one we talked about last summer."

"The God rock."

"That's the one," Jesse said.

"I remember," Sara said.

"Let's go ask Sabrina if she wants to go for a walk," Jesse said.

Chapter Thirty: Most Secret Friend

Most Secret Friend was worried. MSF had not heard from Jack since just after the girl was taken. He had texted, "Done," and nothing since. Now it seemed imperative to communicate. There were things to consider and plan. It was becoming more apparent that after the money was delivered — of which MSF was most certain — there would be no choice about what must happen to Opal, and this was troubling. MSF had not extrapolated this to its now-apparent conclusion, but the idea of all those phone records. . . .

And what was Jack really thinking? They had known each since high school, but their paths had been separate for a decade and more. The reconnection had been serendipitous and quirky; a chance meeting in a restaurant in the old hometown. Jack had offered some unique recreational opportunities in which Most Secret Friend heartily indulged. One thing led to another, and when it became desirous by MSF to kidnap one certain young girl — for reasons both financial and not — MSF knew exactly who to contact and how.

Now, Most Secret Friend was wishing heartily that Jack would contact them. A small — all things are relative — but essential fortune hung in the balance, and MSF was in need of some reassurance about its eminent arrival.

Most Secret Friend keyed in a text and hit "send."

Chapter Thirty-One: Sabrina

There wasn't much conversation in Sara's pickup as it made its way along the route Archer and Tom had followed the night before. Tom drove and Archer rode shotgun until they dipped into a small arroyo that the maps said was the beginning of the crack Archer would follow into the canyon. They paused briefly to drop Archer off. Sara hopped out to take the front passenger seat.

"Be careful," she said.

He gave her a crooked grin and a salute and turned away. She watched him trot away and disappear before getting back into the truck.

With Archer gone, Sabrina and Jesse shared the back seat. Given the extra room, Sabrina pulled out her phone and turned it on. It made several tonal announcements and she listened to messages and then sent a couple of texts. When Jesse inquired, "How *are* things in the outer world?" Sabrian looked startled, and then said, "Keeping up with work," and nothing more. She then sat with her phone in her lap and her arms folded across her chest, staring out the window.

Sabrina was an exotic-looking woman, slender, dark skinned and taller than Sara by several inches. She was 30 years old with a wasp waist and the kind of shape that made most men look at least twice. Helen's acquiescence to the inevitability of divorce started with that body compared to her own rather conventional late-30s frame, which she realized even at the time was a stupid thing to base anything on. But she also knew that her husband was being stupid.

Sabrina's face was narrow and featured a thin, pronounced nose between olive eyes that swept up to the outside corners. When she smiled — not often in recent history — her mouth emulated her eyes and nearly took over her face.

Sabrina had been one of the founders of iTrac, also. She had designed the framework upon which the website operated, and she and her minions were now charged with keeping the site running and safe from hackers, phishers, spammers and scammers. She was chief information technology officer and extraordinarily good at her job.

There were few people at iTrac who made more than she did. One of them was Kelly, who headed up a sales and marketing department with several dozen Fortune 500 clients and several thousand smaller business accounts.

Kelly's earnings were an important part of the attraction for Sabrina. He was also one of the most powerful people at iTrac. That he was intelligent (about some things), innovative, good-looking and stayed fit was a bonus, but those were not her first considerations.

As Opal knew, Sabrina could be fun and funny, but she could also be cold and aloof, which she had demonstrated since they all had gotten together at Delta airport. She seemed detached from the situation, as if observing it from afar. The truth of the matter was that she was worried and angry, and it was partially over money.

When it came time to pony up Kelly's half of the ransom, he was not as liquid as Helen (he'd just spent a few millions on a house in Capolis Beach).

Before Jillian could move a million out of Kelly's account, Sabrina had to move $300,000 into Kelly's account. It seemed to her that some of her choices were going sideways on her, and she didn't much like feeling that way. She had spent enough time in her life wondering what was going to happen next. This latest twist was not setting well with her.

If that makes Sabrina seem shallow, cold and mercenary, two out of three ain't bad, for Sabrina could be cold and she was definitely mercenary, but shallow she was not. She had reasons for her priorities that ran as deep as the canyon they were about to hike into, piled in layers like the sandstone that formed it.

A girl named Rainbow — she never did determine what her real last name might be — took a vow at 13 years old that she would never again live in a place where she could see through the walls, or lay awake on a mattress on the floor waiting for cockroaches to scuttle across her thin blanket. Came a day, she put her best clothes on, took all the cash she could from the drug-sodden people sleeping in that place, appropriated her mother's little .38 automatic pistol and left.

She paid in advance for four nights at a cheap hotel room where she knew they wouldn't ask questions of a 13-year-old wearing too much makeup. She bought food that would last and locked herself in the hotel room and planned her future. She picked a new name — Sabrina, after Samantha's meaner, trickier sister in *Bewitched,* the old sitcom her mother loved for some reason. She chose a last name, Jacqueline, which she liked because it was sexy.

Someone might have suspected she had made that up, but thanks to her mother's nomadic ways, she had just a sub-third-grade education when she left "home." After she tried to rob a San Diego convenience store with an empty .38 auto and leveraged herself into the California State juvenile justice system, she misspelled her new last name to the booking clerk.

How Rainbow, last name unknown — 13-year-old felon, no known address, no relatives anyone could find and Juvenile Hall resident for most of the next five years — became Sabrina Jacklin, CIO of iTrac in Seattle, Washington, is an American success story. After living five years in places with no cockroaches, but plenty of discipline; and where she couldn't see through the walls, or many of the windows for that matter, Sabrina was released into the outside world to live or die on her own.

She had a new high school diploma and the blessings and help of her former keepers. Her parole officer helped her apply for several scholarships, of which she got one: books and tuition at a community college for a two-year course in information technology. She lived close to school, worked as a waitress, kept to herself, kept her nose clean and had her record expunged after a year of good citizenship.

After working at the Hen House Breakfast Haven feeding male chauvinist pigs ham, eggs and hash browns for suggestive comments and lousy tips and eating Top Ramen four nights a week to pay the rent, Sabrina took another vow. She swore that after she got out of college, she was never going to be poor again.

She knocked the IT course dead and continued on a merit scholarship to the University of Washington, where she graduated cum laude with a Masters in IT. She went directly to work for Microsoft. Several years later, she and six coworkers — Kelly included — saw a hole in the Internet that needed filling and iTrac was born.

When someone asked where she had grown up, she told them she was born in prison and grew up in institutions, but managed to escape the system. "It's another life," she would say, "and I never talk about it." Her autobiography began when she turned 18.

So, Sabrina's got some reasons, deep and dark though they may be, for sitting silent and unhappy in the back seat of Sara's pickup rattling across the Uncompahgre Plateau en route to a date with the Mesa Creek trail and some serious play acting.

Chapter Thirty-Two: A Ruckus In The Canyon

Adrian spent a good part of his day scanning the canyon from a spot near the mouth of their hideout, watching for signs that might indicate what he thought of as a breakdown in security. He'd found his way to a small bench where he could see much of the main canyon from below the oasis nearly to the campground as well as a portion of the tableland above. He was not so naïve as to believe there was no plan in place on the other side of the equation. It was his great hope that the plan was to pay the ransom and expect that Opal would be released, which he also knew was almost too much to hope for. Still, for anyone who really loved Opal, that would be the best plan, two million dollars or no.

Nothing moved upstream in the canyon, and only once did he see anything on the upland. A green pickup appeared briefly on the rim road and then disappeared downstream; a bit later, it went back the way it had come. Beginning just before noon, though — P minus 4 hours ("P" being "payday") — there had started a commotion downstream, one that he found distracting and disconcerting. Some group had come down the trail downstream and was hiking up canyon, taking their own sweet time. He reasoned that the green pickup must have left them off.

If the situation had been any other, he would have very much enjoyed watching the three women make their way up Mesa Creek and pausing to play and splash around in any pool of water they came to. They were noisy, playful and, seen through his binoculars, attractive. One even tried to climb every third tree along the trail. Today, though, all he wanted was for them to get the hell out of his canyon and let the end game play out.

It took the ruckus a better part of three hours to finally progress through the boulder field, an inordinately long time. He was relieved when they held a palaver just above the boulders. One of the women repeatedly pointed to her wrist, which Adrian translated as a concern about the passage of time. Body language said they were not exactly in agreement, but finally they began upstream at a more determined pace. Adrian heaved a huge sigh of relief.

A half-hour later, he saw two figures coming downstream and trained his binoculars on them. One he recognized as the man who had been with Opal the morning before. The other was carrying a large red backpack, and Adrian could tell by the way he moved that the pack was heavy. He watched until the two parties met. The men stood aside and let the women pass. Then, he took a long, slow look up and down stream and at the portion of upland he could see. When he estimated that the men with the pack were a half-hour from the drop point, he was also nearly dead certain there was not another living soul in the canyon except them, him, Jack and Opal.

Adrian waited patiently for the two men to arrive at the boulder field. After they set the pack down and began back upstream, he headed for the Tahoe to apprise Jack of the situation. In just over an hour, he was going to be a rich man. Now it was time to consider just how rich he wanted to be.

The Girl Who Wouldn't Stop Running

A***drian was nearly right*** about the number of living souls in the canyon, but there was another, one more — a shadow in a patch of rabbit brush just upstream of the talus slope pouring out of the canyon the Tahoe was hidden in. The shadow had slipped out of the same crack in the rock that the big buck escaped into two evenings before and slid like a rattler down a small arroyo feeding from that crack toward the canyon bottom. Each time the women got loud, the shadow snaked another few yards into the canyon and finally into the patch of rabbit brush, just tall and thick enough to hide a man lying on his belly.

The shadow lay in the rabbit brush and waited for vultures to appear.

Chapter Thirty-Three: "Be Brave, Kid"

T*hough he had watched the money* be delivered from his lookout at the mouth of the canyon, things were not as Adrian would like back at the Tahoe. Jack was insisting that Adrian go get the money and leave Opal in his care. Jack was also insisting that Adrian leave the keys to the Tahoe, "in case she needs to go out," he said. Adrian was highly unwilling to do so.

It had occurred to Adrian that The Contact was probably someone Opal would be able to identify, and that Jack and The Contact were in agreement that Opal would not be allowed to survive this mess. He laid awake most of the night considering alternatives — he couldn't sleep for the snoring anyway — and every pathway he went down except for a couple ended up with Opal dead. Adrain didn't want Opal dead.

On the other hand, having Jack dead was ideal for a couple of reasons. One, it meant more for him. Two, it was apparent that the contact had no idea of who he was. Jack's memory of him was about five years old, and Adrian made it a habit to not refer to any moment in his past that Jack was not a part of. If Jack was dead and the contact didn't know who he was, it meant even *more* for him — *all* the money, in fact. If Opal lived through this, The Contact might get caught, to boot. And maybe he wouldn't. Adrian was willing to take that risk for two reasons. OK. Two million and one reasons — the money and Opal.

But, it wasn't quite time to kill Jack. Opal would hear and know and he didn't want that. He also didn't want to give away the hiding spot — a shot would be heard for a long ways and he hadn't a silencer for his pistol. Of course, there were lots of ways to kill Jack that didn't involve a gunshot, but he wanted to get the money in hand before he took care of that detail. That was the tricky part. It also occurred to him that if Opal was going to get away, she would have to help.

That thought gave him the answer he had been looking for.

In the back seat of the Tahoe, Opal was studying the possibilities the spike offered. She had read that a sharp object and blunt force would cause a car window to shatter, but if she was going to do that, she wanted to be ready to run.

She'd actually slept well the night before, but she'd also had all day to think about her predicament. She too had come to a couple of conclusions, one of which was that these guys — particularly Skinny Man — were not going to let her live. At first, the thought scared her badly, but then she remembered Grandpa Joe once told her, "If you're lost and in a bad way, you may end up dead. But, if you're lost and in a bad way and give in to panic, you will certainly end up dead."

She knew that she was lost and in a bad way, but she wasn't dead yet, which is why she was planning an escape.

She had managed on her last trip out to secure something to hit the spike with, a piece of sandstone she hid in her pants in a very uncomfortable place. It wasn't very large. That meant she would have to hit the spike with every ounce of strength she had and it would have to work. She didn't know what the bad guys would do if it didn't, but she suspected that if they caught her they might tie her up — or worse — which she didn't think about.

She was turning the rock in her hands and trying to figure the best way to hold it when she heard Bad Guy approaching. "Before we go, I'll take her out," he was saying. She stuffed the rock between the seats just as he appeared under the camouflage awning.

The doors unlocked, and he opened the one near her.

"C'mon, kid. Time for a bathroom break."

"I don't have to go," she said.

He leaned in close. "Yes, you do," he said quietly. "C'mon."

"So are you going to shoot me now?" she asked.

"C'mon, kid." Bad Guy sounded truly pained. "I'm not going to shoot you. C'mon."

Opal really did have to go, and she relented. They walked up the canyon and found a spot where she could have privacy. When she was finished, Adrian took back the shovel and began back toward the Tahoe. After a few steps, he stopped and turned back to her. He looked at her for half a minute, and Opal was beginning to think he was going to shoot her. Then he dropped to one knee and reeled her up next to him so his face was right next to hers. Through the holes in his mask, he was looking right at her.

"Listen, kid," he said in a low voice, "and listen good. After we get back to the truck and I leave, untie this rope and count to 900 like this — one-thousand-one, one-thousand-two. When you get to 900, push the door open on the other side quiet as you can and sneak out of the truck. Get away from the truck. Go downstream. Toward the big canyon. Toward the rear of the truck. Find a place to hide and watch. When Jack comes by, wait until he's out of sight and then run as fast as you can the other way — toward the canyon. He'll find out quick you are gone, because the first thing he'll do is come lookin' for you when he gets back. Do you understand all that?"

Opal nodded.

"Be brave, kid. I know you know how. Don't stop being brave."

She nodded again. "Where's my pack?" she whispered.

Adrian grinned behind the mask, and his eyes twinkled. "That's the stuff, kid. Your pack is layin' where Jack threw it, right against the canyon wall behind the truck."

She nodded and they began back toward camp. He put her in the Tahoe, and then went to the other side and opened the far door.

"One more thing, kid," he said in a low voice. "Someone you know has been helpin' us. I don't know who, but someone who knows you and your family has been tellin' Jack where you are. Even after you get away from him, which will be easy — he can't run for sh . . . for anything — you be careful." Adrian pushed the door closed without letting it latch. He saluted her through the glass and disappeared to the other side of the camouflage.

"One-thousand-one," Opal whispered, and stuffed Alice into a pocket in her pants. She began sorting on who might be helping Jack — Bad Guy said his name three times, and she was grateful it was Skinny Man's name that the baggage tag told. She could not arrive at any answer. She thought about that until she got to "One-thousand-three-hundred."

Then she heard Grandpa Joe say, "One thing at a time, Opal." She willed herself not to lose track of where she was.

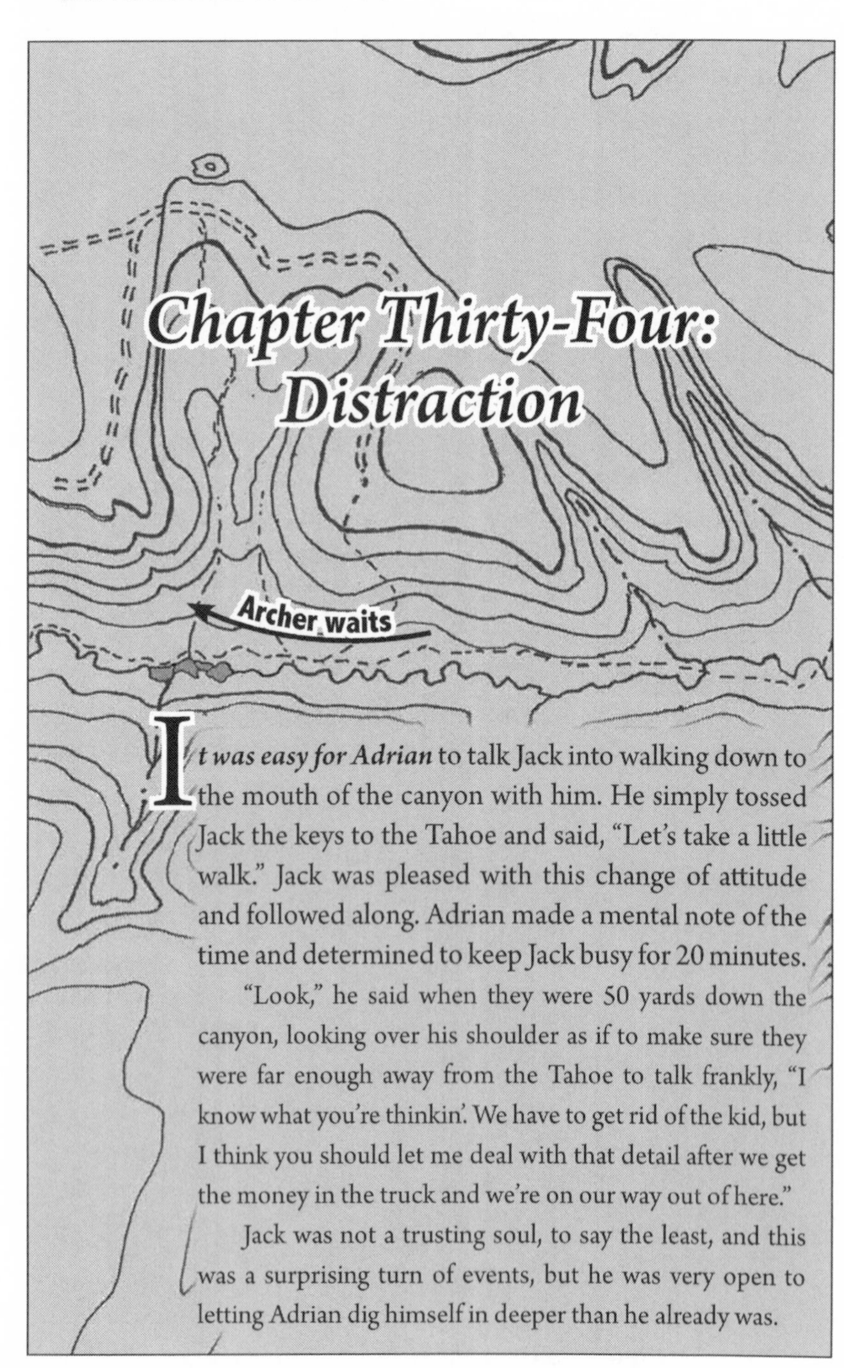

Chapter Thirty-Four: Distraction

It was easy for Adrian to talk Jack into walking down to the mouth of the canyon with him. He simply tossed Jack the keys to the Tahoe and said, "Let's take a little walk." Jack was pleased with this change of attitude and followed along. Adrian made a mental note of the time and determined to keep Jack busy for 20 minutes.

"Look," he said when they were 50 yards down the canyon, looking over his shoulder as if to make sure they were far enough away from the Tahoe to talk frankly, "I know what you're thinkin'. We have to get rid of the kid, but I think you should let me deal with that detail after we get the money in the truck and we're on our way out of here."

Jack was not a trusting soul, to say the least, and this was a surprising turn of events, but he was very open to letting Adrian dig himself in deeper than he already was.

"Let me think about that for a minute," he said.

Not that Jack hadn't already been thinking about things. This was the possible solution to a problem he had been turning over in his own mind for the last couple of days. Adrian wasn't the only one who thought it would be nice to make more off of this deal than a measly half a million. Jack could double his portion and his other partner would be none the wiser. A good opportunity might be one presented while Adrian was dealing with the girl. *Surprise!* Jack thought to himself. *Kaboom.* It was so perfect that it was all he could do to keep from laughing.

He sobered immediately. Jack was always suspicious of the perfect.

"You might be right," he hedged. He wanted more confidence in Adrian's intention. "What's the plan?"

"We roll out of here with the money and a hostage if need be. When we are well away from here, we leave her where nobody will ever find her."

"Where would that be?"

"I'm sure we can come up with a place."

This caused Jack to think of places within a few hours where his own secret part of the plan would also work. And assuming that the other side was going to play fair. . . .

They were approaching the mouth of their hideout canyon and the spot where Adrian had watched for the better part of the day. Adrian looked at his watch. It was almost 4:45.

"I'm going to see if they've cleared out. Hang out here for a couple of minutes."

He clambered up the wall to his lookout and poked his head above the rim of rock. Through his binoculars, he caught a glimpse of the two men who had delivered the money far upstream.

Adrian signaled Jack with a thumbs-up and turned back to watch. He scanned the canyon below for any sign of life. He saw nothing but birds swooping over the beaver ponds. *They must be hunting,* he thought. *I'm gonna learn all about birds when I'm rich.*

Jack watched Adrian watch the canyon, and Adrian let him watch for a couple of minutes past the point where he saw the men disappear into the upper reaches of canyon. When his watch reached a mark at which he figured Opal was out of the Tahoe and safely hidden, he climbed back down to Jack. Grinning, he said, "I'll go collect our pay."

I*n the rabbit brush patch below,* the shadow that was Archer MacClehan did his best to ignore his discomfort and keep the sweat out of his eyes. He'd been in place for a long time, and the sun had not been kind. His willed it to move a little faster and put itself on the other side of the big ponderosa upstream. When that happened, he felt he would be able to move to a sitting position. Now all he had was a line of sight down a small alley in the brush to the trail where it wended past the old beaver ponds, and he wanted to have more of a field of view, particularly toward the hideout canyon. In the dappled shade of the tree, he would feel safe looking out.

As he watched down his alley, a stocky man wearing a ball cap and a shoulder holster crossed his line of sight. *One vulture,* Archer thought.

At that moment, the sun moved behind the tree. Archer resisted the temptation to lift up. It was best to wait for the shade to be complete, but the dream was much in his mind. Where was the other vulture? Where was the coral snake? Most important, where was Opal? He knew, too, that somewhere here was his long-dead grandfather. As he thought it, a raven landed in the ponderosa above him and croaked a raven greeting.

He felt that he had a lookout now. Slowly, carefully, imperceptibly, remembering lessons learned hunting elk and mule deer in the Highwoods above the ranch on Willow Creek, he pulled himself into a lotus position with the crossbow in his lap. He opened his hips, stretched his legs and wiggled his toes, urging blood and feeling back into his feet.

The raven went quiet and the stocky man with the pistol came into view carrying the pack with the money. And then things began to happen very quickly.

Chapter Thirty-Five: Escape

Jack was almost back to camp, happy with the situation as it stood and not even inclined to check on the girl in the Tahoe. Then he saw the tracks in the red dust of the canyon floor. He was not a tracker, but these tracks, dainty as they were, gave him pause. Their improbability and implication at that moment in that place, looking all fresh and new and pointed downstream from the Tahoe took five precious seconds to sink in. He glanced to where Opal's pack had laid for the past day and a half. It was gone.

Then Jack made a huge tactical error. He went to verify what he already knew, that Opal had somehow gotten out of the Tahoe. That took 45 seconds. In those 45 seconds, Opal convinced herself to quit hiding and start running.

She had taken the first hiding spot she felt adequate to the task and tucked herself into a small cove in the canyon wall behind a big juniper and a boulder only 75 yards from the Tahoe. By the time she realized she was too close for comfort, she didn't dare move.

From where she was, she could see upstream, and there was a hole between the juniper and the rock downstream for her to escape through once Skinny Man had gone by. But when he came, his presence paralyzed her. She couldn't immediately convince herself to come out of her hiding place.

This was not a bad thing, although she could not have known that. Jack was, in all honesty, a damned good shot with a pistol. Had she run immediately and had he heard her, there was a very good chance that the race would have been over before it started. As it was, she didn't move until she heard the Tahoe door slam, and then she launched pell-mell down the canyon with her pack bobbing on her back. She considered ditching it, but it had food and water in it. And her cell phone. And now, the spike.

When she came out of the gate, she heard a bellow behind her. "Son of a . . . " The rest of the invective was lost in the echo of the first three words and Opal bolted down the canyon, close to terrified, close to blind flight.

Opal fought it, remembering Jack couldn't run for nothing and that was her chance. While still in the Tahoe, she'd remembered counting her way in with Bad Guy and sorted on how many seconds and then minutes it had taken — almost 40 — and about how fast she could walk — three miles an hour. But it was over rough ground for the last part of the trip and mostly uphill. So she guessed it was a something less than two miles back to where she was taken, which was the only place Opal could think of to go.

But Bad Guy was probably there. She was pretty sure he wouldn't hurt her, but she wasn't completely sure. Opal decided to run downstream when she got to the trail. If she got to the trail.

Opal came to the top of the talus slope that led to the canyon floor. She couldn't run across this jumble, not fast anyway. And it was totally exposed. Anybody at the top had a clear view to the bottom. It seemed like a million miles to the trail.

"Don't give up, Opal. Never give up." It was her grandpa's voice. Where it came from, she didn't know, but it was in her ears. She began down the talus, skipping from rock to rock, boulder to boulder, always on the verge of taking a header, until she knew that to stop was to fall.

When she was about halfway to the bottom and beginning to have some hope of making the trail, something fluttered by her right ear, and she heard an explosion behind her. Then she tripped and tumbled down the rock. She slid hard into a hole behind a boulder and she was very glad she had long pants on. As she rose to go on, big chunks of sandstone showered off the top of the rock and she heard another explosion. She realized Skinny Man was shooting at her.

She cowered then, hiding behind the rock, and all thought of running went out of her. She'd had enough of being brave for the moment. All she could think of was a bullet tearing into her and her blood spilling onto the rock. She couldn't shake that image off. It held her like a rabbit in a snare.

She heard someone moving — clattering footsteps on rock punctuated by labored breathing — and she drew against the boulder she hid behind, tried to make herself flat. And invisible.

A shadow fell into her hole with her, and she flinched away from it.

"So, there you are." Skinny Man's voice was rough and distant. "Come out of there!"

She didn't move.

"Come out now or I'll shoot you right there."

She couldn't see his face against the sun, which was directly behind him. She could see the pistol, though, and it was pointed right at her. She stood up and faced the shadow.

Chapter Thirty-Six: This Better Work

This better work, *Archer thought* and pulled himself up out of his rabbit brush patch. He leveled the crossbow and yelled "Hey!" The man with the pistol turned toward him, and Archer felt the crossbow release.

The steel bolt leapt off the frame of the crossbow, pulling a 3/16th- inch nylon string folded like parachute cord out of a big pocket on the face of Archer's vest. The bolt arced across the 30 yards separating Archer and the other man. The girl in the pink pack took off down slope. Jack turned downhill after the girl and the bolt did as it had in the dream.

It crossed Jack's path and abruptly came to the end of its tether. The cord contacted Jack's legs, and the bolt went hard left, wrapping the cord around Jack's lower legs and tipping him headlong into the rock. The pistol went flying downhill and disappeared.

Archer ran for the downed man and shouted Opal's name, which seem to cause her to accelerate. He shouted her name again as she reached the trail. She didn't even look back.

When Archer arrived at the man with the cord wrapped around his legs, he was struggling to rise, trying to push himself off the rock with his arms. Archer put a knee in the middle of Jack's back, reached for his left wrist and pulled it around behind him.

"I'll break it off if you don't behave," Archer growled. Jack subsided, then convulsed and tried to break free again. Archer straddled him and grabbed his other wrist and pulled it over the first. He pulled a long zip-tie out of a pocket in his vest and used it for a piggin' string. When the plastic strap went tight around Jack's wrists, he gave up with a shudder and went limp.

Archer stood and looked for the girl who had gone streaking down the trail. "Opal!" he yelled. He got no answer. Instead, something solid suddenly poked against the back of his neck, and Archer heard the distinct sound of a pistol being cocked. "Don't turn around," said a voice behind him. "Nice job. Glad you caught the right guy. Saves me some big trouble. Now get down on your knees."

Archer, certain that the object against his neck was a gun barrel, went to his knees on the rock. The crossbow was pulled out of his left hand. A moment later, he heard it clatter on the rocks below him.

"Down on your belly, now," said the voice, "hands behind your back and feet up in the air. Don't try anything stupid and you will live through this."

Archer had no choice, even though he knew he was about to be hog-tied with his wrists and ankles pulled close together. Adrian accomplished that in little time. The bond went tight with the distinctive click of a quick connect buckle and Archer knew he was tied with the sort of webbing strap used on backpacks.

"In case you're wondering why you ain't dead," the voice said, "any friend of Opal's is a friend of mine. Somebody will be along soon and turn you loose, I'm sure. As for this guy next to you, he's no friend of Opal's. Jack, you snorin' bastard, it's truly been a pleasure this time. You want to get up and take it like a man or lay there like a coward?"

Archer couldn't see the gunman, but the first man lay where he had fallen and made no move.

"C'mon, Jack. Answer the question. Or are you too scared?"

The gunman stepped into Archer's view, but he was only visible from the knees down.

Adrian toed Jack's prostrate body. "What? Did you go to sleep again, Jack?" There was no response, and Adrian used his foot to turn the other man over. Jack's mouth hung slack and wide, and his open eyes were unseeing. He was very apparently dead.

"I knew all that sleep wasn't good for your heart, you dumb bastard." The gunman laughed, and it was the same high-pitched laugh Archer remembered from the dream.

"Tell Opal I'm keepin' my promise and to watch out for that other person," he said. Then Archer got the distinct impression that he was alone with what was most assuredly a corpse. He managed to roll onto his other side in time to see a stocky, dark-dressed man disappear upslope with his pack — and two million dollars.

He flexed against the bonds that had him pretzelized, and knew immediately that to do so too strenuously would cut off circulation to his hands. He forced himself to relax as much as possible, wiggled his wrists and felt the strapping loosen just a bit. He stretched back as far as he could and was rewarded with further relief, but when he tried to pull one hand out of the trap, the webbing got tighter.

Archer tried to imagine what the configuration of the webbing was by its feel on his wrists. It seemed to wrap around both seamlessly. Pulling on either caused both to tighten. He flexed back as far as he could, feeling along the webbing, and was rewarded with fleeting contact with the shoulder of a buckle. Try as he might, though, he couldn't pull himself far enough back to grasp the sides of the buckle and release it. After a few minutes of trying, a painful cramp developed in his back and he was forced to relent.

It was hot on the talus and damned uncomfortable laying on his side in the jumble of rock. To make matters worse, a corpse lay six feet downhill, which made Archer loathe to struggle too much. At least Jack — that's what the gunman called him — looked pretty well dead.

Archer wasn't desperate, just helpless, which he didn't like. He knew, as the gunman had reassured him, that someone would eventually come turn him loose. But he also realized it was less than 90 minutes to sunset, that the gunman was getting away, and Opal was by herself with only her phone to guide her. He gritted his teeth and stretched back toward the buckle.

Chapter Thirty-Seven: Waiting

Sara was about to take a chance. Her conversation with Jesse had rambled around in her mind much since morning, landing here and there and making a nuisance of itself. After Tom and Ross returned from delivering the money, she waited until it appeared that Tom was also waiting. Then, summoning up her courage by recalling that she too had been called here by Something-Or-Other and evidently not for nothing, she went and sat next to him where he was sitting against a cottonwood as deep in shade as he could get.

"Tom," she began, "I had a conversation with Jesse this morning." She hesitated.

"About?"

She looked toward the trailhead. "The lead dog."

"AJ."

"Archer. Yes."

"What do you want to know, Sara?"

Something in Tom's voice made her wonder if she wanted to know anything more at all. She realized she could be headed for deep water, where illusion was a life jacket and reality might be lead shoes. Something a counselor in prep school had said as they talked about her relationship with her parents came to mind. "When reality's a big drag, it's best to learn to let go."

Regarding Archer, she wondered if she could do that. In spite of self-admonitions to keep thoughts of the lead dog to a minimum in past months, she'd thought ofhim often. She was not without an image of Archer MacClehan, and the morning conversation with Jesse had proved it not entirely correct. Still, it was he who'd survived her temper by neither retreating nor attacking during the Great Grizzly Adventure. He'd taken care of her devil's club-laden hand. He'd taught her to release her anger into a rock. He'd given her opportunity to remember how much she loved stone and led her across one of the most remarkable mountain landscapes she'd ever been in.

He'd saved her from the bear. And, perhaps most importantly of all, he'd given her opportunity to prove herself brave and reliable. Ready to roll.

She was grateful as anything for all of that, but she wondered now what the other side ofhim might be. She was the girl who'd picked her last boyfriend because she thought he would never surprise her. She'd picked him for his predictability because every other guy she'd ever dated from the time she was 15 turned out to be totally unpredictable. And unreliable. And often unkind. But never unexciting.

Extraction from these relationships always became necessary for survival. It was also always painful and sometimes dangerous — or worse, revolting — when the guy in question suddenly got angry and threatening or needy and desperate. She always found herself running away from them at the end. At least, her last boyfriend had been an improvement, even though he did surprise her. The breakup had been fast and clean and final. He was the one who ran.

So maybe she was getting better at picking who to give her heart to, not that she really ever offered it up to the predictable guy. But part of her heart had already jumped the gap between her and Archer, and she knew the rest was poised to follow. What if Tom were to tell her things she didn't want to know? What if her lead dog image was illusion or worse, delusion. She'd have to run again, and she didn't want to.

These things tumbled around in Sara's mind until the metaphor of the lead shoes washed up against Jesse's Rock. When it did, it was suddenly clear that she not only wanted to know more, she really needed to if she was going to send the rest of her heart to the lead dog. Or not.

Tom was still looking at her expectantly. She took a deep breath and dove in.

"Tell me about Miranda," she said.

"No," Tom said. It wasn't as if he was angry or resistant, it was just that he would not, and he had his own good reasons.

Sara was surprised. She didn't really know what else to say, so she said nothing.

"You know," Tom said carefully, almost gently, "there are things about the lead dog I can tell you. But if you want to know about Miranda, you will have to ask the him." He looked down the canyon. "I know too much to ask. And too much to tell. I think, though, that it will be a remarkably good thing when someone other than me has the guts to ask."

Tom rolled forward and grabbed his knees in his arms, sitting up to look at Sara.

"My guess is that when you ask him, he'll *tell* you.

"Why do you say that?"

Tom leaned back against the tree. "Curiosity killed the cat."

Inside her head, Sara said, *And satisfaction brought her back,* but she kept it to herself. Instead, she said nothing at all and leaned back against the cottonwood.

As she did, a rolling echo came up the canyon and Tom sat up straight.

"That was a gunshot," he said and scrambled to his feet.

"Tom?" Jesse yelled from camp.

The sound repeated itself and Tom ran for his tent. He dragged his pack out and dumped the contents out on the ground. From the pile, he grabbed a black plastic case, a big first-aid kit and a lightweight daypack that had been rolled up.

He shook out the pack and stuffed the first-aid kit in and from the picnic table grabbed a couple of liter Nalgene bottles full of water. And then he was gone, running full tilt down the trail. Sara went to follow but Jesse blocked her way.

"Not a chance, sister. We wait here."

Sara looked after him. She knew Jesse was right, but her heart was pounding as hard as if she'd just sprinted a mile. She turned away. On the picnic table was the black case that had come out of Tom's pack. It was lying near the edge, and she automatically went to secure it. When she picked it up, it fell open. Within it was the distinct impression of a gun, something not quite a rifle but more than a pistol. She held it up for Jesse to see.

"I know what that case holds, Sara, and we can't be of help with what's going on there," Jesse said. "Believe me, Tom is the man to go and go alone."

What neither of them knew was that Ross was gone, too, and several hundred yards ahead of Tom.

Chapter Thirty-Eight: The Best Combination of Events

A*drian couldn't know this,* but with Archer hogtied in the rocks, Tom and Ross headed down Mesa Creek Trail at full tilt and the rest of the group paralyzed in camp, the best possible combination of all events was working in his favor. Toting 65 pounds of money and pack up the talus and then to the Tahoe at 6,500 feet wasn't a cakewalk, but he was strong and the adrenaline factor was set at extreme. Still, he was slowed considerably when the camp came into site and a little unsure of how to proceed once he got there.

Once the two million dollar pack was secured in the Tahoe, though, he talked himself out of tearing out of the place. He dismantled camp instead, being careful to find every last thing he could and stuff it into the space behind where Opal had been prisoner. He took a long look around to see if anything might be left that would be of help to an investigator and then climbed in.

All he had to do was get to the windmill. From there, a gravel road would take him away. But he also knew that he was more in danger of being caught if he just went at it willy-nilly. He took five precious minutes to look at his Colorado atlas, studying roads and terrain between roads. He took a pencil and drew a wandering line across the plateau. He got in the back and pulled out an axe, a bow saw and his toolbox and put them on the passenger side of the Tahoe, just in case. He touched the red patrol pack before he closed the back doors. This made his heart leap. *No more bad deeds, kid,* he thought. *I quit.*

He thought of the last time he saw Opal. She was running directly away from him down the trail at full tilt with her pink pack bobbing on her back. He knew she hadn't seen him coming, and he had stopped himself from calling out to her, which is how he managed to surprise completely the guy with the crossbow. He knew it was the last time he would ever see her, and that made him sad. Opal was the first human being he had allowed himself to care about in he couldn't remember how long.

He wished now that he had kept the crossbow, but he also knew that it was critical to get moving. He climbed in and started the Tahoe. It was, for all of its brute strength, a quiet-running machine. *Sort of like me,* he thought, *the strong, silent type.* He took a deep breath and patted the dash of the Tahoe. "Take me to Bakersfield," he said and pulled the Chevy into gear.

The sound of the Tahoe's engine came filtering down to Archer in the quiet of the canyon. He was stretching back toward the buckle, trying to get past the cramp in his back, telling himself to relax into it. It was as much a matter of will as it was physical exertion, but he was streaming sweat.

When the noise came to him, he had to convince himself to stay calm. He took a deep breath and let it out slowly, stretching back another quarter inch. His goal was to completely relax the webbing bonds and either be able to get one hand out or open the buckle. The cramp returned and he forced himself to go into it. Sweat burned into his left eye and he wanted desperately to wipe it away. A sharp edge of stone pushed itself into his right rib cage. The wave of cramp surged through him and he willed it into the rock that was cutting into his side. When it passed, he took another breath, let it out, stretched back a bit more. The shoulder of the buckle slid an infinitesimal amount more into his grip.

"Almost there," he told himself out loud. "Almost there."

Archer thought of the trussed up corpse lying close by. He was glad to be looking up hill rather than down.

The sound of the engine above him swelled and then began to fade. Archer took a deep breath, exhaled, stretched back a tiny bit more. The motor noise disappeared completely.

Chapter Thirty-Nine: Kelly in a Corner

I*t took Tom a few minutes* to realize there was someone ahead of him on the trail, but he began to recognize a repeating boot-print that overlaid all other tracks. It caused him to pick up his pace, and soon he saw Ross ahead of him in the trail. Tom whistled and the other man looked over his shoulder, then stopped to wait for him.

When Tom caught up, they began down the trail together at a quick march. Ross took note of the weapon Tom was carrying.

"It's been a while since I've seen one of those," he said. "Where'd you get it?"

Tom grew a grim little smile. 'Souvenir of South America."

"Nicaragua?" Ross asked.

"Columbia," Tom said.

"Special Forces?"

Tom hesitated, but then remembered the moment when Ross had not killed Joe on the tarmac in Delta. "Air Force Special Ops."

Tom volunteered nothing else. Ross nodded and asked no more. After that, he just tried to keep up. It had been a while since he had been on a quick march. He made a note to join a gym when this was all over. Which he prayed would be damned well soon. These had been two of the longest days in his life, and he wasn't alone in that.

In the hours of waiting, walking and watching before the sound of gunfire galvanized the camp, Ross witnessed some interesting stuff. Joe and Kelly Skladany had played a cat and mouse game for much of the morning — Joe the cat, Kelly the mouse. It was apparent to Ross, who was a watchful sort, that Joe wanted to talk to his son alone and Kelly didn't want that to happen. They bounced around camp until Kelly was drawn into the planning meeting and Joe sat down at the picnic table with Helen. This seemed to make Kelly very apprehensive. A half-hour later, Joe settled across another table from Sabrina — while Sara and Jesse were Ross knew not where. This drew Kelly right in. A few minutes later, Sara and Jessie approached the table, and Sabrina got up and went with them.

Kelly started to follow, but Joe pointedly stabbed the table with an index finger. Ross couldn't hear what Joe said, but he imagined it to be something like, "You stay right there." Kelly stayed right there, and for the next half hour, there was some serious conversation going on at that table. The others in camp seemed to instinctively know to avoid getting caught up in it. Finally, Joe got up and stalked out of camp, leaving Kelly looking at his hands.

It was a while before Joe came back to camp, after Tom returned from delivering the women and Archer to their walks in the canyon. Joe looked first surprised and then ashamed when Ross told him where they had gone and why. He turned to Tom. "Jesus, Sevlakovs. I'm sorry. I should be doing something more here. What can I do?"

"Listen, friend," Tom answered. "We are all doing the best we can, I figure. Of all the people here, the one who's having the worst time of it is Helen. Next,

I figure, is you. Kelly's numbed to it, it appears. Sabrina's got herself in hand, and Ross, here. . . , well, you seem to have yourself in hand, too."

Ross nodded to that, but he still looked grim. "Joe," he said, "in a few hours, Tom and I are going to deliver the money. The thing you can do for me — for us, I mean — is spend some time with Helen. She's told me often how much she admires you and how glad she is that you and Opal are so close."

Ross looked down the trail, and for a brief instant Joe could see the remorse in him. "It's going to be a long afternoon. Helen needs some comfort and I'm not the one who can give it right now. Nor can she take it from me. You're the best one to sit with her."

Joe looked at Tom. "It's a good call," Tom said.

Joe nodded. "All right. I can do that."

"Thanks," Ross said.

Joe turned to go, and then turned back to Ross. "I got my son in that corner this morning," he said. His face twisted in a grimace. "It was an illuminating conversation."

Ross nodded. "Sorry, Joe. I figured you needed to know, especially in the middle of this, but Helen couldn't tell you. She said you were hurt enough. She's never told Opal the whole truth, either. Doesn't want to get between her and her dad."

Joe nodded and turned away. Tom and Joe watched him walk away.

"What was that about?" Tom asked.

"Family business," Ross said. And that's all he said.

They delivered the money without incident excepting the meeting with the women on the trail. The experience of approaching the boulder field was surreal for Ross. He fantasized that Opal would jump out from behind a rock and yell "Surprise!" as if it had all been an elaborate joke. Instead, it was hot and deadly still and sticky. The only noises were their feet padding on the trail and stray flies zooming by. Neither he nor Tom spoke, and he successfully resisted the temptation to look up for Archer.

At four o'clock exactly, they'd left the pack where Ross had found the note, leaning against the boulder half on the left side of the trail. They simply turned around and began back up the trail. Neither of them dared to look back, but they both felt watched, and they both felt helpless to do anything but walk away.

They'd been back in camp nearly an hour when the sound of gunfire started them back toward where they had been at 4:00. Now, they were just upstream of the boulder field, and they could already see that the pack was gone. They stopped at the drop-off point and Tom took a two-way radio out of his pack and turned it on. He keyed it and said quietly, "AJ. Do you read?"

There was no response. Either Archer hadn't turned his radio on yet, or. . . . Tom didn't think about "or." He keyed the radio once more and repeated the call. Silence.

At Cottonwood Camp, Sara and Jesse heard the call and the lack of response. Both of them also tried their best not to think about "or," but neither was very successful.

"Ask Tom what's going on," Sara said.

"Not yet," Jesse said. She was squinting down the canyon as if trying to see what was happening there. "AJ won't turn his radio on unless it's safe, but someone might hear Tom's. Or worse, have AJ's."

"Dammit," Sara said, right out loud. Her heart was pounding, and she realized she had a death grip on the edge of the picnic table. She forced herself to let go.

Chapter Forty: Reptilian Release

Archer still had his radio. He knew exactly where it was, because for the last half-hour it had been boring into his left pectoral muscle, caught between him and the rocks he was laying on. He had been "resting" for the past few minutes, trying to relax as much as he could after nearly three-quarters of an hour of trying to reach the lock on the buckle. He almost had it a couple of times, but now he was nearly exhausted from trying. The only thing keeping claustrophobia at bay was the thought that Tom was assuredly headed his way. That did not make him any less desirous of getting free.

Once more into the breach, he thought, and began stretching back again. Fresh sweat popped out all over. He said a prayer, not the first one in the last couple of hours.

He took a deep breath and held it. *Five Bears,* he thought, *if you're around, I could use a little help right now.*

Something moved against his left leg then, some animal force. A life form cool and slick settled against the skin of his left calf, and the thought "snake" jumped into his mind. A chill rippled up his body, and it was all he could do to keep from kicking out. He knew it would only make matters worse if he did.

Carefully, deliberately, slowly and with all of his strength, he stretched back. The shoulder of the buckle slid into his fingers. The thing against his left leg moved. His adrenaline level soared and he pushed himself back against the tension in his body and felt the lock mechanism slide into reach. He squeezed, there was a click and suddenly he was free. His legs and arms flew apart and whatever was in his pant leg was launched away from him.

He lay panting on his belly for a half minute before rolling into a sitting position. He stretched his legs out and untangled his hands from the strapping. Just below him, Jack's corpse gaped at the sky.

Sitting on a piece of red sandstone six feet downhill of it was a lizard 10 inches long. It was looking directly at Archer. Its mouth, too, was open and it looked to Archer as if it was grinning at him. It was so macabre Archer could only laugh, out of release and relief as well as the expression on the lizard's face.

"Gramps, if that's you, thanks, but you have a sick sense of humor."

The lizard's smile appeared to get bigger. Then it looked downstream over its shoulder. It looked back at Archer and scuttled off. Archer looked where the lizard had. A quarter mile out, he briefly saw a flash of pink. Opal's backpack! But he was too stiff to even think about going after her.

He turned away from the dead man and took the radio out of his vest. He turned it on and keyed the mic. "Sevlakovs," he said, "do you read?"

Both Tom and Jesse's voices came back. "Are you . . . what's happened, AJ? Are you OK?"

"Hey. One at a time," Archer said. "Tom, where are you?"

"Just downstream of where we left the money. Ross is with me."

"Continue downstream. I'm above the trail on the left. I'll watch for you.

"Jesse, here's my report: One bad guy dead. Other bad guy and money gone. All bad guys out of the canyon — well, sort of — so you can stand down, Tom. Opal's alive and well, but she's also on the run. I think she's totally panicked. Now is the time for someone to call the police."

"Dead," Jesse came back, and Archer could read the shock in her voice. She recovered quickly. "Sara says it's a 45-minute drive to anywhere with cell service."

"Somebody start driving. The guy with the money is still out there. He got started about 40 minutes ago. He can't get off the plateau in 90 minutes, not from where he started." At that moment, the sun dropped behind the top of the plateau, and Archer's hopes dropped with it. Night. It would be dark in an hour, tops. Then it was a totally different game.

"Whoever goes needs to tell the police to put a net around this place," he said into the radio. "Anybody leaving should get stopped no matter what they're driving. Whoever goes out to call needs to keep going to the highway so they can lead the police back."

"Sara says she'll go."

There was no response for a moment. "AJ? Do you read?"

"I read you, Jess. Someone besides Sara has to go. I think it should be you."

Jesse didn't answer immediately. She and Sara looked at each other with similar expressions. "Why not me?" Sara asked.

The radio crackled. "Jess. Did you get that? Whoever is going out needs to go *now*. I think it should be you or Joe. Preferably you. Whoever it is should be on the move and should take a radio with them."

Sara took her keys out of her pocket and handed them to the other woman. "Go!" she said. Jesse grabbed her daypack off the picnic table. "The extra radio is in my big pack," she said. "Top compartment. Be careful." She ran for the truck.

Sara was rummaging in Jesse's pack for the radio before Jesse was out of the campground.

A***rcher was wrong*** about the ability of anyone — particularly Adrian — to get off the Plateau in 90 minutes. Once started for the windmill, he fairly flew across his predetermined route and only once had to veer far to the west to get around the end of an arroyo he had misjudged on the map. He stopped twice to clip barbed wire fences. He was loath to just drive through them. At the second stop, in the growing dusk, he poured all of his extra gasoline into the Tahoe and dragged everything he could find that might indicate Jack had ever existed onto the camouflaged tarp that had covered the Tahoe. He emptied Archer's pack and stowed the money under the back carpet in the compartment in which hundreds of kilos of marijuana and cocaine had crossed the border undetected. He stuffed the pack with all Jack's things that would fit and rolled it and the rest into the tarp. He put the whole load back in the Tahoe, made sure he had left nothing behind and took off.

Adrian arrived at the windmill right at full dark, perhaps setting a land speed record for travel along his chosen route that will never be broken. There he found the gravel road the map had promised and turned right. Twenty-five minutes later, he crossed the Gunnison and five minutes after that, turned left onto Highway 50. Ten minutes later, he pulled to the shoulder and let two police cars with lights flashing shoot by in the opposite direction. Then he forced his heart back into its normal position in his chest, put his pistol back into his shoulder holster and headed for Grand Junction — at the exact speed limit.

An hour later, he was 20 miles west of Grand Junction on I-70 and on his way to Green River, Utah, where he finally stopped and filled up with gas. Then he drove until he couldn't drive any more; to I-15, then north to Tremonton, and then west all the way to Winnemucca. There, he got a room in an older motel far off the interstate. He signed in for two nights and paid in advance — cash.

Chapter Forty-One: Opal On The Run

A*rcher moved stiffly down the talus* to where he thought the crossbow might be and began to look for it. As he did, Tom and Ross emerged from the boulder field, and Tom caught sight of his friend in the rocks above. He waved and Archer waved back. Tom started up the slide.

"I'm going to go look for Opal," Ross said.

"We'll be with you shortly," Tom answered and climbed toward Archer.

If Archer had been paying attention, he might have stopped Ross, but he was intent on finding the crossbow, which he finally did. It was wedged between rocks with a shattered stock. The cocking mechanism was ruined.

He looked the weapon over and concluded that it might be repaired, but he didn't know if he was capable of it. *One shot,* he thought. *I guess that's all it took.* He looked upslope to where Jack's corpse lay in the rock. He didn't look forward to the removal process, but he was certain that the body should be left right where it was for now. The first order of things was to reel Opal in. Ross called out for her downstream where he was slowly walking down the trail, looking from side to side. Archer thought about calling Ross back, but something told him to let it play out.

At that moment, Opal sat hidden a quarter of a mile down the trail in a small niche behind a huge fallen column of the aggregate Sara was so fond of. At least she hoped she was hidden. Her logic had fled her and she was now in an extended state of terror. Skinny Man had tried to kill her so whoever had been helping the kidnappers was going to try to kill her, too. All she could think of was one of the last things Bad Guy said to her: "Someone you know has been helping us."

Who was it?

In a moment of clarion certainty, it came to her. It could only be Ross. He was the one who had asked her to go on this hike. He was the only one beside her mother who knew where she was all the time. He was the one who had brought her here. And he was the only one she could think of who might have reason to harm her, to get her out of the way. Oh and the reasons. She was the only thing that stood between Ross and her mom. She had treated him awfully ever since she had met him. He must have found out her nickname for him. He must have been planning this for months. It had to be Ross.

This was an unfortunate thing for Opal to be thinking at that particular moment, for the first familiar human being she was going to see after escaping Skinny Man was Ross Halliday. And the encounter was going to convince her further.

She heard him coming, calling her name. "Opal. Where are you? You can come out now. It's safe. You're safe, Opal. Come out."

But when she looked there was nobody with him. It was just Ross all alone. She shrunk back behind the fallen pillar.

"C'mon, Opal. Let me take you back to camp to your Mom and your grandpa. C'mon out. It's all over. You're safe now."

Opal had already concluded she couldn't run very well with her back pack on, but she also knew it was imperative to keep it unless there was no other choice. But she made a list of the things she would take if she had to leave it. Water, phone, spike. Alice. In that order of priority.

She had turned her phone on, but there was no phone service. She couldn't call her mom, as much as she wanted, wished, longed to. She texted Most Secret Friend asking what to do. She knew it might take a while for the message to be delivered, and she set the phone on vibrate so nobody would hear if she got a reply.

Now Ross was within a few yards of where she was hiding. She squeezed back against the rock and wished it to be dark, a wish that would be soon granted.

"Opal. If you can hear me, come out. You're safe. It's time to go home." He sounded very sincere and Opal wanted very much to believe him. Maybe she was wrong about Ross. Again. . .

She jumped and nearly wet her pants when her phone vibrated in her hand. She flipped it open and a text appeared. "I am coming to help. Let no one near you until you see me. No one."

She settled against the rock again, hoping Ross had not heard. But he had.

"Opal? Is that you?" She heard footsteps on the rock close by and knew he was coming in her direction. Her adrenaline level was soaring, but she still reasoned that Ross would not be able to catch her even if she had her pack. He was not a runner. Not that she knew of anyway. She gathered up her pack and pulled her feet under her. At that moment, Ross stepped into sight. He was looking the other way, and she shot out of the starting blocks in the opposite direction, directly away from him and downstream.

"Opal!" She hit full stride as his anguished shout reached her, and then she was legging it downstream away from him. "Stop, dammit! Don't run! Opal!"

The last was the same sound he'd made just 36 hours before when he'd first found the ransom note. Once again, Sara Cafferty heard his cry far upstream.

Chapter Forty-Two: Full-On-Scout Cafferty

When *Archer and Tom heard Ross's* distressed shout, they began quickly downstream. Their radios began to crackle simultaneously.

"Archer. Tom. What's going on? Do you read?'

Archer pulled up and got his radio out. Tom went on. "Opal's on the run, Sara" Archer told his radio. "It appears she's really spooked and I'm afraid we're not going to catch her. At least not before dark."

"What do you need me to do?"

Archer thought for a moment. It was just over a mile to the trail the women had followed into the canyon earlier in the day. Archer sighed. *God,* he thought. *How can that only be seven hours ago?* He looked up the north rim of the canyon. In the dream Opal, led by the snake, had run up the canyon wall.

"Whose rig did Jesse take?"

"Mine."

"You'll have to requisition the Explorer then. Can you find your way to the top of the trail you took into the canyon today in the dark?"

"Yes."

She said it with such certainty that Archer smiled.

"I think you might be ready to graduate from Tenderfoot, First Class, Ms. Cafferty. OK. Bring your tent, Tom's tent and enough sleeping bags to go around, Ross included. Meet us at the top of the trail. We're only about 45 minutes out, and you're an hour or more. We'll get a fire together. Grab an extra five gallons of water and food we can eat cold. This, I hope to God, is a one-night camp."

"OK. Anything else?"

"Cell phone. Ask Helen what Opal's phone number is and bring your phone.

Sara touched the notebook in her pocket. "I've already got her number. I asked Helen for it this morning just before I tried to melt down. I'm sorry, Archer. I forgot."

"Don't be sorry," Archer said. "Good girl!"

"I'm not a girl," she answered. "I also got Opal's voicemail password."

"Dammit. Why didn't I think of that?" Archer said. "All right. You're not a girl — or a tenderfoot. Full-On-Scout Cafferty, get under way as soon as possible. Call her as soon as you find service. Maybe you should bring Joe so if you reach her she can talk to someone she trusts."

Sara thought about that for a moment. "I don't think that will work, Archer. Somebody needs to stay with Helen, and I don't think that can be Kelly or Sabrina."

Archer thought that over.

"Good call. Whatever we do, we need to get a message to Opal and tell her that we think a phone friend of hers has been helping the kidnappers. Both by text and voice mail."

Sara, who had been sitting at one of the picnic tables during this exchange, looked up to find Sabrina looking right at her. Sara realized she had been listening for a while.

"I can do that," Sabrina said. "Opal and I are good friends. She'd trust me over a stranger."

"Archer?"

"Yes?"

"Sabrina says she wants to try to reach Opal."

It got quiet for a moment.

"All right," he finally said. "Bring her along. But get started now."

"Yes sir," Sara answered, and somewhere in the back of her mind, she knew that might sound sassy, but she was surprised to find that she was not being sassy at all, that she meant those two words in all of their implications. She was Full-On-Scout Cafferty, and Full-On-Scouts are ready to roll.

"Archer," she said into her radio, "are you sure Opal will use that trail?"

"Pretty sure."

"OK. Thanks. Sara out."

Archer was relieved she didn't ask the obvious question, "What if she doesn't?"

He remembered one more thing. "Sara, do you read?"

"Go ahead."

"Got your running shoes with you?"

"Always a pair in my pack."

"Bring them with you, please."

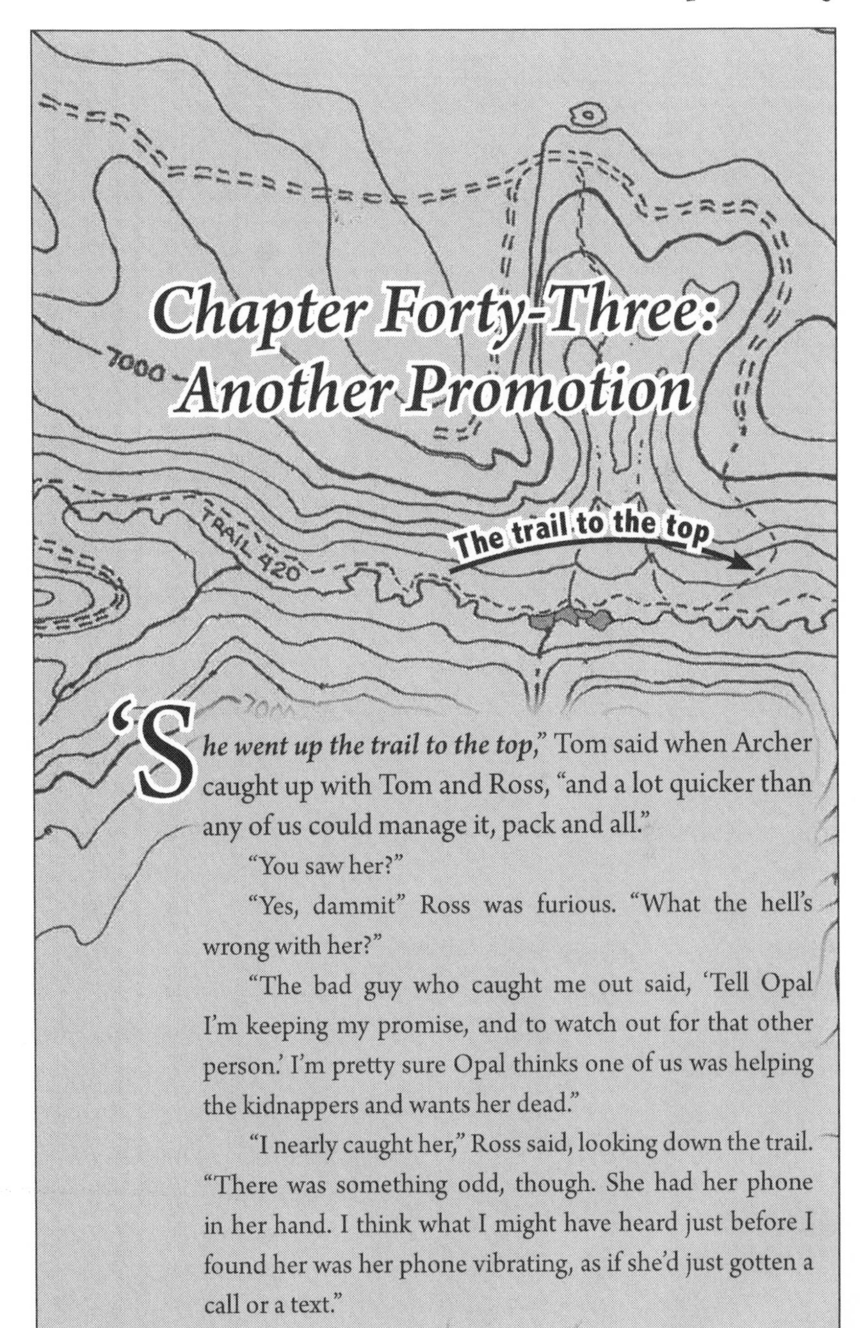

Chapter Forty-Three: Another Promotion

"*She went up the trail to the top,*" Tom said when Archer caught up with Tom and Ross, "and a lot quicker than any of us could manage it, pack and all."

"You saw her?"

"Yes, dammit" Ross was furious. "What the hell's wrong with her?"

"The bad guy who caught me out said, 'Tell Opal I'm keeping my promise, and to watch out for that other person.' I'm pretty sure Opal thinks one of us was helping the kidnappers and wants her dead."

"I nearly caught her," Ross said, looking down the trail. "There was something odd, though. She had her phone in her hand. I think what I might have heard just before I found her was her phone vibrating, as if she'd just gotten a call or a text."

The image of the coral snake came to Archer, and he brought out his radio again. "Sara, do you read?"

"This is Sabrina. Sara's putting things into the Explorer."

"Tell her, first of all, that Opal did go up the trail to the top, so watch for her as you're driving out. Probably to no avail, but just in case. As soon as you get service, call and leave her a message and send her a text telling her that the kidnappers are gone and she's safe to come in. Then, get into her voicemail and see what messages she has — which could be many from friends back home. More importantly, though, I wonder if there's a way we can hack into her text messages."

There was no answer for a moment. Then Sabrina came back, "Probably not, but I'll try to figure out how to forward texts from Opal's phone to mine. Small possibility."

"OK. We're starting up the trail in a few minutes. We'll see you when you get to the upper trailhead. AJ out."

"Sabrina out."

Archer dug into his vest and retrieved his headlamp. Dark was coming down the canyon and they would not top out on the trail before it arrived.

A ***number of miles away,*** Jesse was grinding back toward Cottonwood Campground through the newly arrived night and beginning to hear snatches of conversation on her radio, just not quite enough to figure out what was going on. This wasn't making her too crazy, just a little bit. Overall, she had more important things to think about, like the line of vehicles behind her — no less than five police rigs started the trek, as well as a couple from search and rescue. She kept waiting for helicopters to show up, and they would have except that of two usually available in Gunnison County, one was grounded for maintenance and the other was waiting for first light up near the divide where an injured climber and the rescue team that had gone after her were waiting out the night on a cliff.

There had been some initial confusion about who would respond to Jesse's 911 call, and how they would get there, but it finally boiled down to meeting three county cars, two highway patrollers and the search and rescue rigs at Highway 50. The FBI was still two hours away, and none of the local police wanted to wait for them. Even so, it was past dark when they began back toward the campground, and Jesse was anxious to get there. It had occurred to her, also, that someone should try to reach Opal by phone, but by the time she thought it, she was already well away from camp. She had berated herself for not thinking of it sooner.

As she drew back into radio range, from small snatches of conversation she was getting, she knew that Sara was on the move to somewhere —with Sabrina, maybe? — but it wasn't clear where. She couldn't hear anything from Archer or Tom, but that wasn't surprising, as the radios they had worked pretty much line-of-sight and the men were probably still in the canyon. But where was Sara going?

The flashing lights in her rear view got to be annoying, and she stopped and asked the men in the car behind her to ask the cavalcade to turn their overheads off, which they did. She felt better then, and not quite so pressed to drive faster than she was already, which was about as fast as she dared on the road they were following. Eventually, two police cruisers turned back because they hadn't enough clearance to pass parts of the road and the procession was down to only six vehicles when they finally topped out on the divide road.

It was then that she could hear Archer's radio calls and Sara's answers. She keyed her own radio. "AJ. This is Jesse. Do you read?"

"Go, Jess."

"I've got about six police officers and another half-dozen search and rescue folks following me. Where do you want me to take 'em?"

"Did they set a net around the Plateau?"

"They were dispatching folks left and right when we left Highway 50. So, yes. The net is being set."

Archer didn't answer right away. Jesse could practically hear him thinking. She waited.

"Take them to Cottonwood for now. We don't need them out here tonight. Opal is already freaked out, and I think a huge bunch of folks descending right now would not be helpful. When they do come out in the morning, ask them to make it low key."

"Gotcha. And what do I do with them for the night?" Jesse asked.

"Cribbage tournament?"

"Very funny."

"Sorry, Jess. I don't have a good answer."

"This is Sara. You might suggest they plan out who is going to come out to the trailhead at first light, and who's going to go down the canyon. I suggest that the rest of our party come to the trailhead as soon as it's light. Also, someone will have to retrieve the corpse and the police and FBI will want to look at the site where Opal was taken. Someone will also need to begin investigating the campsite where the kidnappers spent a couple of nights. There were, by the way, some big tracks coming to the road right there when we drove by. Those tracks have to lead somewhere. And, someone needs to make sure the FBI gets headed out in the right direction. As far as food and facilities go, Search and Rescue, my guess, has everything they need for a siege."

Sara let go of her mic key and was greeted by extended silence. "Archer. Do you read?" she finally asked.

A strange voice came back, "Lawrence Averil here, Search and Rescue. If he doesn't, Sara Whoever-you-are, I do. We will henceforth just call you Situation Commander."

"This is AJ. I read you Situation Commander Sara. Sounds like you got another promotion."

"This is Sara. Welcome to the Plateau, Mr. Averil. You may call me Full-On-Scout Cafferty." This made several people in several different places within radio range across the Uncompahgre laugh.

Chapter Forty-Four: Waiting Some More

It was well after dark when camp was made near the upper trailhead. It was basic — two tents, one for Sara and Sabrina; another for Archer, Tom and Ross. The men were to share the watch. Archer was out on sentry somewhere on a point above the camp with Tom's night vision glasses, watching for something, someone, to move.

Sabrina and Ross went to bed, both exhausted from the ups and downs of the day. Tom had kindled a small fire and he and Sara drew up to it, both aware of the unfinished thing between them. Sara kept her questions to herself and waited.

It was very quiet when Tom began to speak. "When we first met, AJ and I, we were just starting high school. I was from a country school where I was the only student in my grade. AJ was new from Bozeman. Other kids knew who we were, but we were each other's only friends for the first month. My dad was a boot maker around Belt. Everyone wore high boots and Poppa was very good at making them fit right. Archer had been summering in Belt for his whole life."

'*Summering*,' Sarah thought. *That's a strange word for this strange man to use.* Her characterization of Tom was not new to her. She'd thought him strange since they first met at a trailhead far to the north, at the very beginning of the Great Grizzly Adventure. The assessment was not unkind. Tom was strange in the way a foreign land is strange, a place with customs, mores and language indecipherable to the casual traveler where the only way to understand the place is to move in and stay for a while.

Tom had his arms wrapped around his knees in front of him. He let his legs go and stretched out and leaned back on one elbow as if he was releasing something — his story, perhaps.

"AJ and I seemed to be made for each other — and still do. Sometimes, it feels like we've been part of each other since before we were born. We are not incomplete without each other, but we are more complete with each other."

He paused. Sara was looking away — far away, it seemed.

"I'm listening," she said. She was thinking too, and what she was thinking was that if Tom wasn't strange — foreign — he'd never be able to say such a thing to her. Intimacies such as these between American men were seldom acknowledged, much less spoken.

"The day we met, we were in the school yard at the high school. I stepped into a fight between him and three others. AJ had won a round by knocking one boy down, but the three of them were about to jump him. I evened out the odds, I guess."

"Have you always been very strong?" Sara asked.

Tom then did something that surprised Sara, endeared him to her and made her laugh heartily for the first time in several days. He pulled himself into a lotus position, made muscles with both arms, clinched his fists above his head and said something in a Slavic tongue.

"What?"

In a heavy accent, he said, "Seence I was leetle boy!"

He joined her laughter.

"Where were you a little boy?" she asked.

Tom grew a faraway look. "Near Klaipeda, Lithuania. A place called Juodkranté on the Curonian Spit." he said. "We immigrated when I was four."

Sara did a little math. "Before the Soviet Union dissolved."

"Yes. As you say." There was much more in those four words, but Tom's tone said there was no more he would say about that.

"The summer we got out of high school, at the end of June, we said goodbye for a while. I went to work for the Forest Service on a fire crew. He was at Colorado Springs for his doolie summer. I didn't know what to do. Montana State was waving a football scholarship at me, but something or other told me that wasn't the way to go."

"Something-Or-Other?" Sara asked. "With a capital "S?"

Tom looked at her and smiled. "As you say. Yes, with a capital "S."

"Instead, I went to the Marines in October when the Forest Service laid me off, but they didn't take me because I was too short for my weight, by half inch. In December, I was working in the hardware store in Belt. AJ came home from the Academy. We stayed up all night and talked." He paused.

"Miranda, too?" Sara asked.

"Yes. Mira, too," Tom said, from far away.

"Mira." Sara said.

"Mira. It was her nickname. It almost means 'peace' in Russian, you know. Just one little extra vowel. Maybe it is the female 'peace.' Russian is a funny language that way." He was still in the distance. But then, he laughed. "It was her idea."

"What was?"

"That we should stretch me out so the service would take me."

"What?"

"We knew the Marines wouldn't give me another chance, but we thought the Air Force might. All we had to do was make me a half-inch taller for long enough to get measured, and I was in. So we came up with this contraption that stretched me out."

"Stretched you out." Sara said.

"We called it the rack, but it was really very comfortable. We took an old Formica kitchen table and bolted a piece of half-inch plywood to it. Then we tied a foam pad to the table and I got on. AJ and Mira strapped my ankles to the table and then they tilted the table toward my head until the plywood at the head end hit the floor — about a 45-degree angle — and I took a nap. It actually felt good. About an hour later, they stood me up and measured me. I was an inch taller. About 30 minutes later, I was still a half-inch taller. At one hour, though, I was back to normal."

"Normal." Sara laughed.

"Yes. Normal as I could be, anyway. We tried a couple of different timings, but the results didn't vary much. So, we knew that I had to be measured within a half-hour of getting off the table.

"So. We make an appointment with the recruiter in Great Falls and I go talk to him and get everything lined up for a physical. When I go to take the physical a few days later, we borrow a horse trailer from Mira's dad and put me on the table in the back — with everything I can get on, because it's 5 below — and we drive to the induction center. My physical is at 10 a.m. At 9:55, we pull up in front of the building. At 9:57, I stand up and walk in. The sergeant has all my paperwork ready. I walk in, strip down — which took a few minutes in itself — get weighed, and at 10:20, I get measured. No blinking. Just go to next station. I was in."

"And, then?"

"Eight months later, I was in the Air Force SERE program, being trained as a trainer. Then, I was tapped for Special Operations and that's where I served for almost six years."

"Explain please."

"SERE stands for survival, evasion, resistance and escape, special training that every pilot gets, and every AFSOC enlisted man. Air Force Special Operations Command is like the Army Special Forces, only better, of course." He laughed. "Not really. Similar training, but somewhat specialized. Among other things, we were trained to be downed pilot rescue specialists."

"So, did you rescue any downed pilots?"

Tom grew quiet, and Sara feared she had overstepped a boundary. The image of the black case on the picnic table came to her, and with it a thought that maybe Tom might rather not talk about this. Finally, he looked at her and nodded. "A few," he said, and Sara knew that was all she would get from him about that. And maybe all she wanted.

"Did you and Archer see each other at all while you were in the service?"

Tom nodded. "We saw a lot of each other — especially for the last three years I was in."

Sara saw the question coming in her mind, surrounded by orange and red flashing lights. She tried the brakes, but they failed and she slid right past the warning signs and into the intersection of her thoughts. *Holy samoley!* she thought and tried to swerve, but the question came rocketing out. "So, where were you when Archer was discharged?"

Sara had never seen Tom look quite so surprised as when her question hit him, and she wanted it back desperately.

Dammit! she thought. *I don't know enough to keep my mouth shut. When will I learn to just be patient?*

"Yeah, Tom. Where were you?" Archer's voice came out of the dark before them and Tom and Sara both jumped with surprise.

Archer came into the light of the fire, and Sara was surprised — and relieved — to see that he had his crooked grin on.

Tom looked down into the fire. "I was waiting at the gate to take you home."

"Took us quite a while to get there, didn't it?"

"It did," Tom looked up and grinned. "I was telling Sara how I got into the service."

Archer laughed. "The rack! I hadn't thought about that for a while. Mira's dad's horse trailer. Man, it was cold that day." He sighed. "That was a long damn time ago."

"It was," Tom said.

Archer handed Tom the binoculars. "Thought I saw something move out east about an hour ago, but nothing since."

Tom took the binoculars and grabbed his daypack and disappeared into the dark. Archer sank down by the fire.

"How you doing, Ms. Cafferty?" Archer asked.

"Fading, Mr. MacClehan," Sara said. "But, better than some of the others, surely."

"True. There are some anxious folks out there in the dark."

"You're not?"

Archer gave a short laugh. "I gave up being unduly anxious long ago. Opal's fine right now, I think. She's scared, lonely, maybe hungry and thirsty. She's a canny girl, though. Her grandpa's taught her a lot about being in wild country. My guess is that she doesn't know who to trust — number two bad guy gave me a message for her — 'Tell Opal I'm keeping my promise, and to watch out for that other person.' But I think she's safe and tomorrow we'll catch her."

"Catch her. What do you mean?"

The dream came to mind. "Running Woman is stronger than the snake and can run longer than the little one," Five Bears said. "She and the little one will both stop running." He thought of telling Sara about the dream — about all the dreams, for that matter — and it was a good thought; a welcome thought. But he knew it would be when Tom and Jesse were there, too.

"Remember what I said this morning — or maybe a hundred years ago — 'sometimes logic is not all we have to work with?' "

"Yes."

"When this is all over and the four of us are alone together somewhere, I will tell you what I meant by that."

Sara had no doubt about what he meant when he said "the four of us."

"Alright." She said. "I can wait." She also remembered what Tom had said. She screwed her courage to its utmost limit. "Will you tell me about Mira, too?"

Five Bears' final words came to Archer. "To catch Running Woman, you must stop running. A broken heart does not mend in the dark."

Archer grew a faraway look and stared into the fire. Sara held her breath until he finally said, "Yes. I'll tell you about Mira."

Sara reached out and put her hand on Archer's arm.

"Scoot in here, girl," he said, inviting her closer.

"I'm not a girl," she said, though she felt very much like one at that moment.

"Scoot in here anyway," he said. And she did.

Chapter Forty-Five: The Girl Who Wouldn't Stop Running

Far to the west in Winnemucca it was just lightening along the eastern rim when Adrian finally went to his room. He sat on the edge of the bed and argued with himself about what to do with the money, bring it in or leave it where it was. He decided it would be much more prudent and practical to leave the majority of it in the hiding place in the Tahoe until he got someplace with assured and absolute privacy and had a better place to stash it.

Adrian was actually somewhat amazed at how clearly he was thinking about all this. As he drove across Utah and into Nevada, he had begun planning how to filter his new fortune back into circulation. He also followed out all of the possible threads he could think of originating from the kidnapping that might lead to him, and most all of them were bundled up in the tarp in the back of the Tahoe. The last ones were the tires on the truck, which had left some very distinctive tracks across the plateau. The items bundled in the back were either going to be burned in a small canyon in the Mojave that he knew about from previous adventures or disbursed into a series of dumpsters. When he got to Bakersfield in a few days, the Tahoe was going to get some new shoes. They would be much quieter than the old ones, he decided.

Adrian finally lay down. He looked at his watch. In just over an hour it would be 48 since he had plucked Opal off of the Mesa Creek Trail. He missed her, and he hoped she was OK.

"No more bad deeds, kid," he said aloud and closed his eyes. He was asleep in two minutes, and there was no snoring to disturb his rest.

About the time that Adrian said "No more bad deeds, kid." Opal woke with a start from a dream that Bad Guy was telling her just that. She swam out of sleep and found herself not in the Tahoe, but in a small cleft of sandstone with a perfect early morning view of Ross's Explorer parked beside two tents. There was no human in sight,

She still didn't know what to do, but she knew she would get no more advice from Bad Guy — or Most Secret Friend. It had been nearly dark when she topped out on the tableland, and she had cast around for a good place to hide and found her little spot. Just after that, her phone had gone dead.

Shortly after her phone died, someone came and camped close to where she was hiding, but she resisted all temptation to go see them because of Most Secret Friend's last message. "I am coming to help. Let no one near you until you see me. No one." Also, even in the dark she was sure it was Ross's Explorer that brought the people to the trailhead. Now she could see that she was right, and Ross was still her prime suspect as kidnapper's helper.

She wasn't sure how Most Secret Friend was going to save her, but she didn't know who else to trust except her Mom, Dad, Sabrina or Grandpa Joe, and none of them were around, or at least she didn't think so. From the niche she found in the hill above the trailhead, she could almost hear what they were saying in the camp but not quite. They built a fire, and she could see them coming and going around it. They set up two tents. Opal knew that they weren't actively seeking her, but after a while, a person with a headlamp came from the camp and went up on the hill above her. They didn't come back, and she reasoned they were watching for her.

She stayed very still and prayed that Most Secret Friend would show up before they found her.

That is not what happened.

A half-hour before sunrise, a person got out of one tent and began walking up the hill toward her. It was a woman Opal had never seen before, of slender build with red hair. She was on a direct line toward Opal's hideout, as if she was purposefully coming to get her. Opal waited and tried to be invisible, but she knew that the woman was going to see her. Barring some miracle, she was going to walk right up to her little spot.

Opal laid her pack aside and tucked Alice into the outside pocket. She picked up her full Nalgene and the spike. She'd finished her trail mix already. She prayed the woman would change course. She did not. Then right above her hiding place, she heard movement. Someone said, "Good morning," a male someone. It was Ross!

The woman raised her hand in greeting, and as she did, her eyes locked on Opal's. They flew wide with surprise and Opal fled. The woman, now behind her, shouted something like "Archer!"

Ross bellowed her name, but Opal was off like a shot to the east, where there appeared to be no road on which anyone could use a car to catch her. She would run downstream along the edge of the canyon toward the highway she knew was out there somewhere. She ran hard for two minutes and then slowed and settled into the cadence she loved, the one where all troubles fell behind. She lengthened her stride, determined to beat her own best time at whatever distance she had to run to get to that highway and somewhere she could call Most Secret Friend. And her Mom. And the police.

Chapter Forty-Six: Coral Snake

R*oss watched Opal sprint away* with a sinking stomach. He'd nearly stepped on her. If he had been paying attention. . . . why would she run from him? Again. He wanted to kick himself for not seeing her sooner, for not bringing Helen or Joe out here. Mostly he wanted back that invitation he had issued — he looked at his watch — just 60 hours ago.

There was Opal's pink pack in the little hole she'd popped up out of. As he reached down to get it, the woman Sara went running east out of camp, and he intuited she was going to try to catch Opal. *Good luck with that,* he thought. Sabrina was rummaging in the tent she had shared with Sara. Archer was now above him watching the girl through binoculars. Tom was looking west, talking to his radio. He was getting no response.

Ross walked numbly toward the Explorer, unsure of what to do. He set Opal's pack down. The back compartment was unzipped. Inside was her cell phone. "Jesus," he said and practically tore the pack getting it out. He flipped it open and found it dead, but the charger was in the Explorer. He jerked open the door, plugged the phone in and it powered up. He keyed into the text messages, and read the last one from someone called "Most Secret Friend," and a chill went through him.

"What'd you find?" Archer asked from behind him.

He showed him the text. "This is the last one, the one she got yesterday when I found her in the canyon."

"Do we have service?" Archer asked.

Ross nodded.

"Put it on speaker phone and dial that number."

The phone on the other end rang four times before the answering service picked up. "Opal. Sabrina here. Leave me a message."

"What? Where is she?"

"Out there," Tom said from behind them. "She took off after Sara and the girl."

"That ain't good," Archer said. "Dammit."

The radio came to life. "Archer, Tom. Do you read?"

"This is Tom, Jess. Where are you?"

"Just topped the grade above Cottonwood. With everybody, including family. Forty minutes out, I'd guess."

Archer held out a hand. Tom gave him the radio. "Does any of your crew have horses?"

"None with us. What's up?"

"Opal ran again this morning. Sara and Sabrina are in pursuit, but there's a big complication. I need something that can go off road faster than a human."

"This is Lawrence Averil, Search and Rescue. How about a Honda Trail 90?"

"I'll take it. Thanks. Jess?"

"Jesse here."

"We have Opal's phone, and we're pretty sure we know who's the helper now. It isn't good. So put the guy with the motorcycle out front. Averil?"

"This is Averil."

"Drive as fast as you dare."

Jesse was doing social math at high speed, but coming up empty. "AJ. Who's the helper?"

"I'd rather not say. We're pretty sure we know, but give us a few minutes to look further."

"Gotcha. See you soon."

The further they looked, the more it became apparent to Archer that Sabrina was the coral snake. She'd been communicating with Opal for the entire time Opal, Ross and Helen had been traveling, and for months before that, often commiserating notes and calls of support in response to Opal's complaints about Ross and, more recently, the vacation plans. She'd received enough information to be of significant help to the kidnappers.

Archer waited impatiently for Averil and his motorcycle. Tom didn't. At Archer's suggestion, he began off across the desert at a dogtrot, following the tracks left by the three runners. He knew he wouldn't catch them while they were still running, but he also knew that long after they hit the wall, his would still be in front of him. He kept his eye on the trail and trotted into the rising sun.

Archer looked after him until he was out of sight, and then turned his attention to the west, watching for a sign that the others were coming. A ways out, he could see a dust cloud rising and took comfort in that. But he was worried and willed them to come faster. If Sabrina was the coral snake — and he was now convinced that she was — not only was Opal in danger, but Sara.

He thought of their time by the fire the night before. It was the first time in a long time that he'd kept that sort of warm company with a woman. His heart and soul were thrumming with an odd and intense combination of emotion: grief and joy confronted simultaneously.

Not a girl, indeed, he thought.

"Hurry up, dammit," he told the dust cloud.

Chapter Forty-Seven: Pursuit

Sara had been slow to react beyond yelling for Archer because she was wearing her boots unlaced with no socks when Opal materialized in front of her. When the girl bolted, she thought for an instant about going after her barefoot, but knew it would be disastrous. Instead, she galumphed back to camp and ripped into her pack for her shoes. Everyone was out of the tents, and Archer was running up the hill with binoculars in his hand.

Sabrina stared after Opal. "What are you going to do?" she asked Sara.

"I'm going to try to catch her."

"I'll be right behind you," Sabrina said. "Go."

It took Sabrina about two minutes to dig her shoes out and get them on. By that time, Opal had a half-mile start and Sara was out nearly a quarter mile. Sabrina grabbed two liters of water, which she knew would slow her down, but she knew Opal's skills. It could be a long race, and she wanted to be there for the finish.

It *was* a long race. In open terrain, with only sagebrush and rabbit brush to dodge around, Sara was able to keep Opal in sight much of the time, though in the beginning, Opal was out of sight often. It was good for Sara that Opal had shed her jacket and had a white t-shirt on. And it was also good that Opal was wearing pants instead of shorts. It slowed her a bit and protected her legs from the prickly, thorny stuff she was running through. It was the slowing that was important to Sara, who saw in the first half hour that she was gaining on the girl, but not at a rate that said she would catch her in an hour. It would be at least two.

And it was.

If Opal had been able to run straight line, she might have made it to the river, but the canyon edge was not a straight line. There were places where she was forced away out to her left and then drawn back to her right by terrain. Sara just stayed on Opal's tracks and Sabrina stayed on Sara's, easy to find in the dusty desert surface. All three were running over their heads, across terrain not built for optimal running. Underfoot varied from solid rock to soft sand. At fifteen miles, they were all approaching the wall. Sara reasoned that Opal would hit hers first. She hoped. She prayed. Because she could see hers out there not too far. Just beyond Opal, in fact, who was not far ahead any more.

Sara was right. Opal was now fighting fatigue as well as terror. Whoever was chasing her was getting closer. She could hear footfalls behind her as strong as a heartbeat. She searched ahead for a place she could veer into and hide.

A few hundred yards out, she saw a depression in the ground that signaled the beginning of one of the arroyos that fed the main canyon. If she could get in there, she might find a little crack to get into. But she had to get there well ahead of whatever was behind her. She went inside and found the chunk of reserve her cross-country coach always told her about and turned on the afterburners.

Sara couldn't believe the girl in front of her was suddenly accelerating away from her. She had been close enough to start looking for a place to take her down with a flying tackle, a spot somewhat softer than a slab of sandstone. Now the gap between them was growing, and Sara was certain she wasn't going to be capable of closing it quickly. She had reserves left, but not the kick she was seeing Opal make.

It occurred to her, though, that this might be Opal's finishing kick, that this could be the last leg of this desert marathon. She could let Opal win. All she had to do was finish. But where was the finish line? She knew the answer as soon as she thought the question. Opal was headed for the lip of a little side canyon, now just 150 yards away.

That could be good, but it could be bad, too. Some of these little cracks grew into a major side canyon that led clear down to Mesa creek, but many ended with a drop into the main canyon that was often 200 feet or more. She couldn't tell which the arroyo might be, and there wasn't time to figure that out.

"Opal!" Sara yelled. "Please stop."

Opal disappeared over the edge of the arroyo.

Behind Sara a quarter mile, Sabrina plodded grimly along. After two hours at full tilt, she had given up trying to catch the other two and now tried to just keep them in sight. She could still see Sara, but Opal had disappeared. Opal had disappeared before, though, as had Sara, but Sabrina had managed to find them again by just following their line of tracks. Then, Sara disappeared.

Sabrina jogged on toward the edge of the canyon.

Chapter Forty-Eight: Cornered Wildcat

T*he arroyo Opal threw herself into* in desperation was of the second variety. It gradually dropped a quarter mile toward the canyon wall and then became a slot in the sandstone. A few hundred yards after that, it narrowed to only a few yards wide and then dropped abruptly 100 feet to the main canyon floor. There were several fingers out of the slot to the left and right. When Opal reached the end and found herself trapped, she skittered back to the nearest finger and scrambled into it, climbing blindly until she hit a 15-foot wall there was no getting past.

She put her back to it and searched for help. Just below her was a boulder big enough to hide her, and she got behind it just as she began to hear her pursuer in the main part of the slot. She was calling for her, and Opal gripped the spike, the only thing she had left. She had dropped the water bottle long before.

Sara came to the 100-foot drop, and was relieved to see Opal's tracks reverse. She followed them back to the crack Opal had gotten into.

"Opal?" Sara said. "Are you in there?" There was no answer.

Sara moved slowly into the little crack, watching for possible routes out. When she reached the point where the wall was in sight, she stopped. The only place Opal could be hiding was behind the boulder on the left side. Sara approached slowly, all the while talking to Opal like one might a frightened animal.

"Opal? I know you're in here. You're safe. You can come out. You're going to be fine. It's all over. Your mom and dad and Ross are waiting in camp. Come out, please."

Opal came out full force, over the top of the boulder just as Sara came abreast of it, spike in her right hand raised to strike. She leapt like a cornered wildcat right over Sara, hit the ground hard and scrambled to her feet. Sara tackled her from behind. Opal was strong and twisted in Sara's grip to face her. She kicked with both legs and Sara's grip was loosened. Opal found her back against the sandstone wall. Sara came to her knees right in front of the girl, and Opal thrust at her with the spike. Sara tried to knock the big nail out of the girl's hand and got a punctured palm for her trouble. Sara backed away and Opal launched herself into her, driving the woman back hard. Sara's head snapped back against rock, and she saw shooting stars. She went down in a heap. Opal pulled away and scrambled back toward the main arroyo.

Opal rounded the corner and began quickly back up the slot canyon, but saw a shadow moving above her. Someone else was coming! She reversed and searched for another option, another way out. There was none. She found herself trapped at the edge of the world. She grimly gripped the spike and waited.

S***ara came back to consciousness slowly***. She rolled to her side and got her feet under her. She stood, shaky and near exhausted. Someone called for her and Opal in the main canyon, a woman's voice. Though echoes distorted the voice, she intuited it was Sabrina.

"I'm here," Sara answered.

Sabrina appeared below her. "Where's Opal?"

"Somewhere out in the canyon, I think." Sara was still foggy from her collision with the rock. "Watch out for the spike she's carrying."

"She won't hurt me," Sabrina answered. She turned away. "Opal?" she called. "Opal, it's Sabrina. Come on out, please. Let's go home."

Sara took a step after Sabrina and sat down hard. Her head really hurt. She was dizzy. Sabrina disappeared around the corner, and her voice receded into a jumble of echoes. Sara tried to stand and found it easier to stay on all fours. She crawled toward the main stem of the canyon. When she came to it, she was practically run over by the lead dog.

"Holy Samoley, girl. What happened to you?" Archer dropped to one knee beside Sara and attempted to help her up. She waved him off.

"Not ready to stand," she said. "Banged my head. Dehydrated. Exhausted. Not a girl."

"OK, woman. Let me see. Are you bleeding?" Archer gently felt the back of Sara's head and found a sizeable goose egg but no blood.

"Not bleeding," he said. "Where's Opal?"

Sara moved to a sitting position. "Sabrina went after her. If you didn't pass them, they are that-a-way. They can't have gone too far. There's a big drop a ways downstream."

"Here." He handed her a water bottle. "Stay here. Tom's not far behind."

Archer stood and moved off downstream. Sara watched after him and was surprised to see in his right hand a small automatic pistol. Somehow, that didn't make sense, but this had been a nonsensical morning. For some reason, she looked at her watch.

It wasn't even nine o'clock yet. Mountain Time.

Chapter Forty-Nine: An Arrest

W*hatever Archer expected to see* when he began down the canyon with a pistol in his hand, it wasn't what he found. Instead of one of the scenarios he imagined involving the coral snake and the little girl, he found Sabrina and Opal in embrace, sitting near the edge of the drop Sara had told him about. Sabrina sat with her back against the canyon wall, and Opal was practically in her lap. Both of them were crying and Sabrina was cradling the girl's head and rocking her back and forth.

Someone behind him said, "What the heck?" Tom had caught up.

"I don't know," Archer said. "Something's not making a lot of sense."

"Amen," Tom said.

Archer tucked his pistol away and Tom secured his weapon as well.

"I have to check on Sara," Archer said. "Keep an eye on them."

"It's OK, Opal." Sabrina said over and over again. "It's all over and it's OK."

But, it wasn't all over. Not for any of them quite yet.

Sara sat quiet, nearly drowsing as Archer tended to her wounded hand. At the same time, he was trying to sort out what to do next. It was a long way back to camp, and he was unsure of what to do with Sabrina — or Sara, for that matter. Both of them and Opal were exhausted and he was worried that Sara might have a concussion. Though it was tempting to think Sabrina was not the coral snake, he knew her comforting Opal could be some sort of remorseful reaction on her part. He didn't want to give Sabrina a chance to get away, but he was also reluctant to truss her up in front of Opal. The girl had suffered enough trauma in the last few days.

Finally, he led everyone out of the canyon and was further convinced of Sabrina's innocence when she insisted on staying beside Sara, who was understandably moving a bit slowly.

"Boy, can you run," she said to Sara, causing Sara to smile weakly.

"Not right now, I bet," she answered.

Once up out of the slot, the radios Tom and Archer were carrying came on strong with calls from Jesse and Averil. Archer waited for a hole in the noise and then keyed his mic. "Jess, Averil, do you read?" They both came back immediately and Archer continued, "Listen carefully, please. You may tell all concerned that Opal is safe and will soon be back in camp. All is well here. Both Sara and Sabrina are fine, and Tom is keeping an eye on things. That is all I have to say about that and we can discuss further complications when I get back to camp. Do you read me?"

Jesse came back, "I read you, AJ. No more questions, correct?"

"Correct," Archer said. "Hang on a moment."

He turned and squatted in front Opal, who was sitting beside Sabrina on the ground.

"Hi, Opal. Do you remember me? I'm a friend of your Grandpa Joe."

"You're the pilot, right?" she answered shyly.

"That would be me. AJ MacClehan." He held out his hand and Opal shook it. "It's been a rough couple of days, huh?"

Opal merely nodded and Sabrina put an arm around her. Archer could see that Opal was still a ways from collapse, but he wanted to be sure she was strong enough for what he had in mind.

"So, do you think you could ride back to our camp on the back of a motorcycle. Your Mom and Dad and Grandpa Joe are waiting there."

Opal looked at Sabrina and Sabrina nodded. "OK," she said. "I can do that."

"Good girl." He keyed his radio again. "Jess. Averil. I'm bringing Opal to camp. If there is some sort of cross country transportation available for the others, it would be much appreciated."

"This is Averil. Can you give us a location?"

Tom had already checked his GPS. He keyed his radio and rattled off longitude and latitude.

"That's a location, alright," Averil responded. "Transportation on the way."

Archer left Tom in charge of the two women and put Opal behind him on the back of Averil's motorcycle and headed for camp. When he was half way there, the helicopter that had rescued the climber that morning flew over on the way pick up Tom, Sara and Sabrina. They all arrived at camp about the same time.

If Archer was convinced by those moments at the end of the chase that he was mistaken about who the coral snake was, the FBI was not. Using whatever investigative magic they had at their disposal, the agency had already found that the phone number of Most Secret Friend was indeed that of Sabrina Jacklin of Seattle, Washington. In addition to hundreds of texts and calls made between that phone and Opal's, there were an inordinate number of calls and texts to a number with a New Mexico area code, including several on each day leading up to and the day of the kidnapping. Calling that number led to a voice-mail box with the following greeting.

"This is Jack. Leave a message and I'll get back to you."

When the agent in charge asked later that day who Jack might be, both Archer and Opal were able to tell him: Jack was the dead guy in the talus.

About two o'clock in the afternoon, Sabrina was arrested as an accomplice to kidnapping. She was incredulous, and then angry, and then hysterical as they put her into handcuffs and an FBI vehicle.

The people there to witness her arrest who could not believe she was guilty were Archer, Sara and Tom. Opal, thankfully, was already gone from the Plateau and on her way to a medical clinic in Delta. In a sense, though, it was Opal who had sealed her fate. When asked who Most Secret Friend really was, first by an agent and then by her mom, she had to answer, "Sabrina."

Chapter Fifty: Solution and Absolution

T***he Skladany kidnapping spent two weeks*** at the top of the charts before it began to fade from the internet, national news and public consciousness. The tale had a happy ending — sort of — with a macabre twist. Accused was the girlfriend of the kidnapped and then rescued girl's father.

It took a month before the FBI team working on the case became finally convinced that Sabrina was a victim of identity theft. Someone had gotten into her life electronically and established a credit card in her name, which they used to buy a phone and open a cell service account — and keep it current. The investigation was continuing.

Helen, Ross, Kelly and Joe changed phone numbers to protect their privacy. Opal got a new phone. The FBI had taken hers as evidence. Kelly went home completely troubled, first by his girlfriend's apparent duplicity; second, by reverberations of a conversation he'd had with his father sitting at a picnic table in the Cottonwood Campground. He didn't try to contact Sabrina, even though she tried several times to reach him.

After being taken first to the clinic in Delta and then to a motel, Opal slept for 24 hours straight, and her mother with her as Ross and Joe stood watch against the press. Then, Opal and Helen flew home to Seattle in the Citation — on Kelly's dime. After a really good physical and a visit or seven to the therapist, Opal was determined to be pretty much all right; though Helen and Ross both noted she was more serious and quieter than she'd been before, and possibly more respectful. Opal and her mother agreed that Opal would stay at Helen's house for a while, until things settled down at least.

Helen found a good tutor and Opal began home-schooling, which, when she returned to school for the spring session, put her even farther ahead of her classmates.

After holding Ross responsible for her kidnapping and finding out he was not, and after his expression of joy and gratitude at seeing her when she arrived back at the camp on the back of Lawrence Averil's Honda 90, Opal made her peace with Ross. It was a good peace. Once she opened up her heart a little bit, he moved right in, and she found there was space for both him and her dad. In different rooms of course.

She didn't talk to anyone except her mom, Ross and her therapist about her time in the Tahoe or the prelude and aftermath of her imprisonment. She would eventually tell her Grandpa Joe about most of it, and how his voice in the background had saved her life and sanity. But that would be when she was about to graduate from college ten years hence.

When asked by anyone, including the FBI, she said not much about Bad Guy, except that he was careful with her and helped her escape, even though she knew that he was a very bad guy.

Sabrina went first to the county jail in Grand Junction and then to the federal lockup in Denver before finally being released a month to the day after Opal was taken. Sara, Tom and Archer, after witnessing the end of the chase, were all sure she was innocent, and they kept in touch. Sara drove across the Rockies from Montrose to meet Sabrina when she got out.

Sara found her understandably shaken, angry and completely at a loss about what to do next. She certainly wasn't going back to Capolis Beach. Nobody at iTrac had tried to contact her. Kelly owed her $300,000. She poured this out to Sara, who advised her to follow her instincts about Capolis Beach. She didn't know what to tell her about iTrac, but counseled her to inform iTrac's president of the situation and let the chips fall where they may. By the time Opal went back to school for spring session, Sabrina Jacklin was back at Microsoft, temporarily $300,000 poorer, infinitely wiser and consummately angry.

The anger would fade over time. She and Opal reconnected in April when Opal called and asked her if she would come watch her run in a cross-country meet. Later that summer, they ran a half-marathon together. But not with Kelly.

Archer, Tom, Jesse and Joe flew back to Montana two days after Archer toted the girl back to the trailhead. Their jubilation at saving the girl was tempered by Sabrina's arrest and the apparent fact that the guy with the money had gotten clean away. He was an x-factor, and not a person involved besides Opal knew anything more about him than he was real and he had a red backpack with two million dollars in it. And, he drove a beat-up Tahoe.

Even after the FBI identified the corpse as Jack Armstrong, drug runner and small-time thug, there was not a single connection they could find to anyone but Most Secret Friend, and even that connection was severed when it became apparent that Sabrina was not MSF. The trail of the money and the man who took it evaporated near a windmill by a gravel road to which sheriff's deputies followed his tracks.

Sara took a deep breath to clear her head and continued in Colorado with her research. Her phone time escalated remarkably, though. Archer, for the first time in his life, consented to get a cell phone, even though there was apparently no service at his house on the Short Creek Road. He could, though, type in a text at home and hit "send," and sometime later he would hear the "I just sent a text message" sound.

This always made him smile.

Chapter Fifty-One: "Keep It Simple."

N*either Sara nor Archer advertised* their escalating relationship. It didn't seem necessary. Or appropriate, for that matter. At least not yet. There was a lot of work to do, and they were doing it. Slowly the story of Archer and Mira and the tragedy between them came out, and Sara listened intently. Slowly the circumstances of Sara's growing up came out, including her banishment to boarding schools and expensive summer camps by her distant parents, which Archer could no more understand than the man in the moon, but gave ear and sympathy to.

While all this talk went on, fall continued toward winter and just after Thanksgiving, Archer asked Sara if she would come visit for Christmas. Her semester of research was ending. A descending snow line was chasing her off the Uncompahgre.

She took a deep breath and said, "Yes."

A few days later, Jesse was walking down First Avenue in Three Bridges on a set of errands. She happened to glance inside as she passed the jewelry store, and what to her wondering eye did appear but Archer MacClehan leaning over a counter in the vicinity of the rings.

Several thoughts collided in her head at once, some painful, some not. In her mind's eye, though, she saw a small shape out on the horizon rising and falling rhythmically in what she recognized as a running cadence. It came closer and soon she recognized it as a woman, a slender woman with red hair and fair skin. She was running not just toward Archer, but toward her and Tom and the others who lived in this place as friends and neighbors. It was a powerful figure, slight though it seemed. It would change things when it arrived. How, she couldn't know, but Something-Or-Other told her to open her arms.

She slipped into the shop and went to stand beside Archer at the counter. He looked up, surprised, caught out. She didn't look at him, but into the case. She studied the rings, and said, conversationally, "You and Sara been talkin', huh?"

"Hours," he admitted.

"Have you told her about Mira?"

"Some. Enough. Enough to know . . . "

Jesse slipped her hand into the crook of Archer's arm and pointed into the case.

"Keep it simple, Mr. MacClehan," Jesse said. "Nice and simple. Sara will like that."

Chapter Fifty-Two: "No More Bad Deeds, Kid."

T*hree days after Christmas* was a breakfast gathering at the MacClehan house on Short Creek. Tom and Jesse trooped in as Archer brought a cast-iron pan out of the oven filled with a golden-brown breakfast egg pie.

Tom had a paper in his hand, which he held out to Sara and pointed to a headline in the "Northwest" section, "Seattle Woman Arrested in Skladany Kidnapping."

The subhead read, "Family banker implicated by computer records."

Sara skimmed it. "Holy Samoley." It came out of her one syllable at a time, well spaced.

"What?" Archer asked.

Sara read the article out loud.

" 'Seattle banker Jillian Dumas was arrested Friday as a suspect in the kidnapping of Opal Skladany, a case that held national attention last September. Dumas was implicated when a cell phone received in the mail by the FBI in Denver provided a link between her and a purported kidnapper, Jack Maxwell, who died during the rescue of the girl in Colorado. It was also learned that Dumas and Maxwell attended high school together in Albuquerque, New Mexico.'

" 'The phone, which was mailed from a downtown San Clemente, California, post office, was accompanied by a hand-written note that read "Sabrina didn't do it," a reference to Sabrina Jacklin, who was arrested initially in the case but has since been released. FBI spokesman Will Admire told reporters that evidence found on a personal computer owned by Dumas indicated she had used the identity of Jacklin, for whom she was a financial advisor, to establish and maintain a phone relationship with the victim. Dumas, who has entered a plea of not guilty, is being held on a $1,000,000 bond.' "

Sara pointed to a picture of the suspect. "Look at her. She's gorgeous! What do you suppose her motivation was?"

For Archer, the last bit of the dream fell into place. It had been the one part he couldn't reconcile, especially after Sabrina was exonerated. Now he understood.

"A coral snake," he said.

"What?" Jesse asked.

"Good analogy, Mr. MacClehan," asserted Sara. "Very beautiful. Very dangerous. Interesting."

Tom looked at Archer then, for Sara had used the word with the identical inflection that a girl named Mira once had. Archer looked hard at Sara and then out the front window. He had on his best crooked grin and Tom could not help but join him.

"Do you suppose that's the banker friend who put the ransom together?" Jesse asked.

They found after breakfast that such was the case when Joe and then Ross called to fill them in. It was coming out on television and the internet that Ms.

Dumas had some very expensive habits that had left a large hole in a trust fund she was responsible for.

"But where's the money?" Jesse asked after Ross had hung up.

"The two million dollar question," Sara said. "Whoever sent the phone must have it all."

"Bad Guy," Archer said.

"What?" Jesse said.

"That's what Opal called the other kidnapper." Tom said. "Jack Maxwell was 'Skinny Man' and the other man was 'Bad Guy.' That came out as she was explaining things to Sabrina at the end of the chase. She was babbling, going off. And Sabrina just sat there and held her. I knew she wasn't guilty right then."

"I hope Sabrina's OK," Sara said. "She's pretty tough, but she's been through a lot."

"She and Kelly are kaput?" Jesse asked.

Sara rolled her eyes. "I wouldn't mention his name in front of her. When she was arrested, he bailed. She and Helen are on better terms than she and Kelly. Kelly's the outcast in that world."

"He's got some big fences to mend," Archer said. "For Joe's sake, I hope he'll get to it."

"But where's Bad Guy?" Jesse said. "It seems to me that we need to find him."

"We?" Sara asked.

"OK. Somebody. It would be a shame if he gets away with it."

"He did save Opal's life," Tom said.

"I suppose," said Jesse, "But he also put her in grave danger."

"You're right," Archer said. "But if not for him, Opal would be dead and Most Secret Friend might never have been caught."

"Still," Jesse said. "Two million bucks."

"I know," Archer said. "Unfinished business."

He was looking out the window above the kitchen sink, wrist-deep in dishwater. Sara happened to be looking at him and saw something pass across his face, a shadow like she had seen at other times, one that meant something she knew not what. She touched the new ring on her left hand with her left thumb. She wondered if she would ever get used to it being there and she wondered if she would ever know what those secrets were.

Archer turned from the sink and dried his hands. "Speaking of unfinished business," he said, looking directly at Sara, "I think it's time for the four of us to have a talk."

W***hile Archer and his "team"*** gathered 'round the kitchen table, far to the south, Adrian DeMill unlocked Desert Motor Sports for the day. He'd opened the shop six weeks before and somewhat to his surprise, it was getting busy. It was surprising to some of his customers that Desert Motor Sports had *Audubon Magazine* in the waiting room, but they were still bringing their four-wheelers, motorcycles and desert rigs to him to fix or modify.

Adrian had been very careful about setting up the business and acquiring equipment, always buying good used and always paying cash with an assortment of bills. Soon, he had a checking account into which he deposited checks and cash — ostensibly from customers — on a regular basis. Adrian was, he thought, as happy as he'd ever been in his life.

He'd found Jack's phone in the Tahoe while he was removing the restraint cage during an extensive remodel carried out in the very private paint room at Desert Motor Sports. Adrian reasoned that when he'd bundled up the camp — long since disposed of — and piled it into the back of the Tahoe, the phone had fallen out of the pocket of a coat Jack had left on his chair. He did a little research and determined to mail it to the FBI office in Denver, which he did, taking extreme care to insure it couldn't be traced back to him. He knew it was a huge risk, but he also understood that it was important to Opal and her safety.

After he dropped the small package into the collection box outside the San Clemente post office, he drove away in a newly painted Tahoe with some very good — and very quiet — all season radial tires. He made his way past the place where the little house had been and found it covered with a condominium complex. He considered going up into the hills to the gate with his last name on it. It had been in his mind since his return to Bakersfield, but it was also in his mind what he had promised Opal.

He came to an intersection and stopped. A right turn took him up into the hills. A left turn took him back to Bakersfield. He looked up the road to the right and said aloud, "No more bad deeds, kid."

Being careful to signal, he turned left.

The End.

More books from Blue Creek Press →

About Blue Creek Press

Blue Creek Press, based in Heron, Montana, produces proprietary as well as subsidy books. Blue Creek Press also writes, designs and produces collateral materials including brochures, maps, booklets and newsletters for private enterprise and nonprofits. Blue Creek Press offers publishing services that are client-oriented and reasonably priced.

www.bluecreekpress.com • books@bluecreekpress.com

Books from **Blue Creek Press**

Order from your local bookstore, online at bluecreekpress.com, amazon.com, or contact books@bluecreekpress.com

Hunting Tigers (and Other Adventures) on Christ's Service in Old India.

A double-barreled tiger gun, newspapers and Lysol may not seem the tools of missionaries, but they served Herman and Mildred Reynolds well as they ministered for two decades to the Gonds of India in the last years of British occupation. ***Nonfiction. 180 pages.***

Four-Eleven! Pulaskis, Planes & Forest Fires

by Rich Faletto

A memoir of trail maintenance, fire fighting, and flying on the Wenatchee National Forest. Rich brought his manuscript and dozens of pictures to this project, and Blue Creek Press helped him through the design, production and printing process. What we put together is a fine adventure story of life as a summer employee of the United States Forest Service in the mid-1960s.

Buy* Four-Eleven! *online at www.four-elevenstore.com

Run, Naomi, Run! ***by Pauline Shook***

Naomi Milner saw no grand destiny for herself, just toil and travail and trouble. Before her thirtieth year, she moved to a raw Nebraska homestead; buried sister, father and brother; married a man she didn't love to escape another she despised; and made three places home in newly-settled Washington State and Idaho. ***Fiction, 240 pages, Also available in hardbound.***

Other Books by Sandy Compton

Side Trips From Cowboy: Addiction, Recovery and The Western American Myth

Explore the Nez Perce trail — and a path to recovery from addiction — with a Western writer and traveler. Half memoir and half adventure story, it is also written to illustrate to addicts and non-addicts alike the nature of addiction as a spiritual disease — and what one might do about it. ***Nonfiction. 320 pages..***

Archer MacClehan & The Hungry Now

The first Archer MacClehan adventure is set in wilderness, where things happen fast and life is often served raw. That's how the Hungry Now, a grizzly who's lived a long time by paying attention, likes *his* dinner. Follow Archer MacClehan and four other hikers into the Skyrocket wilderness and meet the bear, who changes everybody's life — some a little and some a lot. ***Fiction, 180 pages***

Jason's Passage

In *Jason's Passage,* Jason Indreland brings Caleb and Sarah Blascomb the healing thread of a past miracle in their lives and later brings a message of hope, love and commitment from them through six decades and two generations to their grandson Alex. Come meet two generations of Blascombs by way of *Jason's Passage.* ***Fiction, 120 pages***

The Friction of Desire

Dr. Mary Magdalene Miller, a not-so-Freudian analyst, is the narrator of this funny, fast read about Larry Longquist and his search for clarity. Hilarious, touching and pertinent to the world we live in. You'll want to read it again. Watch for more from M.M. Miller, M.D. in the near future. ***Fiction. 182 pages.***

Caleb's Miracle

Ten-year-old Caleb Blascomb is hero of a winter ride through 1889 Montana and a meeting with a family in trouble. Caleb's faith, his father's resolve and "El Carim," the mysterious fourth "wise man" save the day. Color illustrations throughout by Sandpoint, Idaho, artist Sally Lockwood. A book to read to children. ***Fiction. 32 pages***

Made in the USA
Middletown, DE
22 December 2021